The Art of Friendship

Romance Arts
Book 4

Amanda Hamm

ISBN: 978-1-943598-17-5

The Art of Friendship is a work of fiction. All names, characters, places, events, etc. are products of the author's imagination or are used fictitiously.

1

The door slammed, and the sound was immediately followed by a surprised yelp. Audra appeared from around the corner looking apologetic. "Oops," she said. "I didn't mean to push the door so hard. I was excited, and it got away from me."

Violet was in the kitchen finishing her dinner when her roommate arrived. "Why are you excited?" she asked.

"Logan's going to help me with my plan," Audra said. "It'll be perfect."

Violet turned to put her empty plate in the sink behind her. She tried to project calm as she turned back to get details. Audra was on a self-assigned mission to pair Violet with the right guy. Violet kind of wanted the help, but Audra's last attempt had fixed Violet up with the wrong guy and strained several relationships until a big misunderstanding was straightened out. It was only natural to be nervous about a new idea. "What plan?" Violet asked.

"I think Katie and Cameron will make an awesome couple. I'll get her to meet me for lunch tomorrow and Logan will ask Cameron, and the two of them will be on a double date with us before they know what hit them."

The plan did not involve Violet. There was serious disappointment that Audra's matchmaking had found another target. Apparently, she wasn't as nervous as she thought. But she was amused that the plan involved Audra's boyfriend. "How did you get Logan to help?"

Audra smiled with a sappy expression. "It was easier than I thought actually. It seems he likes to do stuff for me. I'm so lucky."

Impossible to argue that point even if there hadn't been a knock on the door at the same time. "I'll get it," Violet volunteered. Audra was still holding the bag she usually stashed in her room after work. And she'd want to take her shoes off.

"Thanks." Audra dashed towards her room while Violet moved towards the front door. "But don't say anything if it's Katie."

Violet just laughed at the unnecessary admonishment. She wouldn't interfere with Audra's big plan. Audra knew that. It was Alison at the door anyway. "Hi, Alison."

Alison came in rubbing her hands together. "Cold tonight."

"Yes, it is." Violet waved her inside to shut out the nippy wind. The sun had set and November was a week away. It was definitely getting cold. Why did that thought cause her to imagine putting on the sweatshirt Ryan had been wearing last week? Violet pushed that thought aside to focus on her guest. "How's your big project coming?"

"Awesome." Alison's eyes brightened with the subject. "I sent him some pictures of what I've done so far, and he loved them. He told me to keep going."

"That does sound pretty awesome." Violet stepped towards the table with Alison as they talked. Alison worked in her family's shop restoring and selling furniture. Most of her work involved repairs and basic refinishing. But last Friday she'd been gushing about a customer who asked her to get creative and make a one-of-a-kind table for him. She was carving designs in the legs and on the surface. He intended to have a piece of glass cut to fit the top.

"I want to see the pictures, too!" Audra burst from her room just before Violet could ask.

Alison beat them both to it as she already had her phone out and was bringing up the pictures. She turned it towards Audra as Violet leaned over her shoulder. "This is the bottom of the first leg. And this one," she quickly swiped to a new picture, "is what I did around the edge before he committed to the entire surface."

"Nice," Violet said, with emphasis.

"Yes. I love that the grooves are not all the same depth," Audra said. She was an artist, a painter, and it wasn't surprising she had a more specific comment.

Violet just knew that she liked it.

"Okay. Katie will be here any minute," Audra said, switching topics in an unnecessarily hushed tone. "I'm going to ask her to come look at my paintings tomorrow so I can take her to lunch afterwards. Logan is meeting us there with Cameron. Try not to say anything that'll make her suspicious."

"Or you could have just not told her," Violet pointed out.

"Alison doesn't want to be left out, especially since I need to use her store in my plan." Audra's art hung at the furniture store.

Alison did seem entertained by the plan. "Do you know something?" she asked Audra.

"What do you mean?" Audra sounded confused, but there was something in her eyes – the way they danced back and forth – that said she knew exactly what Alison meant because she did know something.

Violet shared a smile with Alison before she pressed for more information. "Did Katie tell you she's interested in him?"

"I... think they will be good together."

"That didn't answer the question," Alison said.

"*Why* do you think they'll be good together?" Violet asked.

Audra opened her mouth but closed it before any words exited. She paused to rethink, then said, "I think that after my plan works, *Katie* will have an interesting story to tell you."

"Oh." Violet didn't want to wait, but she heard what Audra was saying, that there was something Katie had asked her not to share yet. She and Alison respected that. They may not have had time to find out anyway as another knock signaled Katie's arrival.

Audra moved to let her in while Violet grabbed the Tichu cards and brought them to the table. She'd been Alison's partner last week so Violet took the seat next to Alison to mix it up.

Katie typically spent most of her lunch breaks at the restaurant where Audra worked, but Audra hadn't seen her at all that week. Chastising her for that lapse was the first order of business. It turned out that Katie's boss had her doing some lunch hour overtime to prepare for a meeting no one wanted to attend. There was no way to give her a hard time after that explanation. Audra simply offered her a seat.

The ladies' Tichu night had been set up by Audra and Violet a few months ago. First, they had to teach Alison and her mom. Then they replaced Alison's mom, at her request, with Katie and had to teach her. As the more experienced players, Violet and Audra had not yet been on the same team. That's why Violet was mildly surprised when Audra claimed the seat across from her. But they had given Katie several weeks to learn, and she was clearly very sharp. When no one questioned the arrangement, Violet began to shuffle.

"Okay. I have an idea," Audra said.

It appeared she was not going to waste any time before beginning her matchmaking. Sure enough, she asked Katie to check out her work just before noon – which was when Audra stopped showing the paintings for the day – and get lunch afterwards.

Katie did not immediately answer. Her expression suggested she was waiting to hear what was behind the invitation. More evidence she was a fast learner.

"It's a good idea," Audra said, sounding more defensive than encouraging.

"It is," Alison said, "which makes it odd that you sound like you're making a hard sell."

Violet smirked at the jab at Audra's lack of finesse.

Audra ignored it and forced nonchalance into her voice as she said, "Do you want to come or not?"

Katie agreed and seemed fine with waiting a day to figure out what was going on. All four women focused on sorting their cards for the first round. Alison and Katie did very well and ended Violet's concerns about putting the novices together. Not that she'd been all that concerned. She turned to Audra as Alison dealt out a new round. "So how was your day at work?"

"It was pretty... oh!" Audra had begun to nod as she thought about her day. Her eyes widened, and she momentarily froze as a thought hit her. "Except you guys won't believe what Addie said today. She hasn't been there very long but long enough that..." Audra cleared her throat and backed up to the beginning of her story. "I was in the kitchen when things were quiet before dinner. It was a good time for me to get something to eat, and I was talking to Ryan. Addie came in as I mentioned that I was going to catch Logan on his way into the guys' Tichu game tonight. Ryan told me I better not make him late, which I just rolled my eyes at. Then Addie asked me who Logan is. When I told her he's my boyfriend, her eyes kind of bugged out for a second before she looked really confused. She said, 'I thought you guys were married.' It took me a second to realize she meant *to each other*. She thought I was married to Ryan."

There was laughter at Audra's outraged reaction. Katie was the first to be able to talk. "Well, you two run the restaurant together, and you have the same last name," she said. "It's not a completely ridiculous assumption."

"I suppose not," Audra conceded. "Except that first of all... ew. And second of all, I don't know how she missed all the times Ryan has mentioned that I'm his sister. Sometimes it feels like he wants everyone to think that's the only reason I have the job."

"It is kind of…" Violet paused to make sure she wasn't about to reinforce the slight Audra expressed. "Ryan didn't ask you to work for him in a nepotism sort of way but because he knows you well enough to trust you to do a good job. That's not a bad thing."

"What did Ryan say about being mistaken for your husband?" Katie asked.

"Nothing," Audra said with a shrug. "I think he wanted people to think he was too mature to care."

Violet thought he was too mature to make a big deal out of a simple misunderstanding. And even though Audra was his sister, she was beautiful. She had long blonde hair, a dazzling smile and an hourglass shape. It was difficult to imagine any guy being offended at being linked to her. There wasn't a ton of family resemblance. Ryan also had blond hair, though his was darker. Audra's was darker near the roots so perhaps this was only because he kept his short enough that it didn't have time to be affected by sun. They both had blue eyes. Though the shade was similar – like the aquamarine gems on a bracelet in Violet's jewelry box – they were still very different. Audra's eyes squinted and bulged and danced with every thought and emotion that passed while Ryan's gaze remained steady. The mystery of what lay behind it pulled Violet in every time.

"I'm trying to decide if I'm brave enough to call Tichu," Alison said.

Back to the game. Violet could tell by her hand that other people had all the best cards. She said nothing rather than risk revealing that Alison probably didn't have anything to worry about.

"Go for it," Katie said. "One of us should be brave at some point, and I'm not sure it's going to be me."

Alison nodded. She succeeded in her Tichu call and extended the early lead she shared with Katie.

They talked about how many trick-or-treaters they might expect and some of the costumes they'd worn as kids. Violet told the story – though Audra had heard it before – of the year she'd dressed as a giant Christmas present and how proud she was of her costume until she realized it was nearly impossible to climb porch steps in it. A few rounds passed while they talked. Some better luck put Audra and Violet in the lead and gave them the eventual victory.

Audra was leading the others towards the door before Violet had the cards back in the box. It might have been the first time they walked next door without anyone suggesting it first, but it was about time they stopped pretending it was a novel idea. Audra's brothers, Ryan and Trevor, lived in an apartment on the other side of what all used to be one really big house.

The guys played Friday night Tichu with two friends, one of whom was the guy Audra was dating and the other was the guy she planned to fix up with Katie. The guys' game had been going on much longer and was part of the reason Audra had wanted a game for her friends. The guys didn't talk as much and usually powered through two games in barely more time than the women played one. Audra used to check in on the guys – bringing Violet along – and continued to do that when she realized she had time to play and still check in.

Audra also had a habit of ringing the doorbell to announce her arrival before letting herself in. Trevor could not seem to resist commenting on it, which was probably why she kept doing it. Siblings did not always bring out the best in each other. Violet entered next to Alison, who was dating Trevor.

"Nice superfluous use of the doorbell," he said sarcastically before greeting Alison in a much happier tone.

"Tomorrow at two?" she asked.

He nodded and reached out to squeeze her hand before she turned to leave again. Alison never stayed to watch. Trevor seemed to take the game most seriously of all the guys, and she didn't think he'd appreciate having her around as a distraction. He'd never said that, but he hadn't tried very hard to encourage her to stick around either. Based on the admiration shining in his eyes as he watched her go, his focus would suffer with her nearby.

Violet chanced a look at Ryan. He was looking at his cards and not back at her at all, let alone as though he was happy to see her. She sighed. Yeah, she sighed like a lovesick teenager and not a twenty-two-year-old adult. It just seemed that *everyone* around her was finding happiness in love. Her sister was even getting married in a little over a month. The closer she got to attending that wedding alone, the more Violet was becoming glad Rosie was planning a pretty boring reception. It wouldn't be so bad to not bring someone to hear the speech she was supposed to write but hadn't started.

Her sister had given her a lot of instructions. Violet was supposed to talk about growing up with Rosie, citing specific memories and how they illustrated qualities that would be important in a successful marriage. She was not allowed to share anything embarrassing. The speech should be entertaining but not funny. It should be heartfelt but not sappy and brief without being too short. Violet wasn't sure anyone could thread those needles. She told Rosie she was expecting the impossible and that perhaps she could just write out exactly what she wanted Violet to say.

That had not gone over well. Rosie cried. She'd been feeling overwhelmed because the florist had just yelled at her – she was now using a different florist – so it hadn't really been about the speech. But it still made Violet feel bad, and she was resigned to writing something even if it was disappointing. She hoped it would at least also be forgettable. Five or six speeches were planned, and Violet was second. Surely at least some of the guests will have zoned out by the end of the first one.

"Still a game going on here."

Violet jumped at the sound of Trevor's voice. Speaking of zoning out. It was a good thing she was only watching. She looked at Logan, expecting him to be distracted by Audra. But Logan was focused on his cards and not Audra, who was studying the scores of previous rounds on his phone. Cameron tossed an eight onto the table. Cameron was the one not paying attention? That was new.

Violet positioned herself where she could see Ryan's cards over his shoulder. It was more fun to follow the game from the perspective of a player, and she liked hiding behind him anyway. She didn't feel invisible if she chose to be out of sight. Logan grabbed the cards when the score had been recorded. He always shuffled, even when it was someone else's turn to deal, even when that person was perfectly capable and likely to shuffle more anyway. Violet wondered if this was some sort of superstitious thing or just a bad habit. It usually didn't bother anyone too much.

She chatted with Katie and Audra about some of the tricks between rounds. As long as they kept quiet while the hand was in play, the guys didn't mind commentary. In fact, they enjoyed the possibility that they would be praised by…

"I wish I knew if those tens were gonna win," Trevor said. He sounded impatient again, and it was Cameron's turn again.

Why was Cameron distracted? And why was Audra smirking about it? Maybe it wasn't Katie who expressed the interest that sparked her matchmaking plan. Maybe Cameron said something to Logan. Violet shifted her attention to Katie. She was watching Cameron's cards. Was that because Logan and Ryan had been claimed and Trevor was cranky? Or did she appreciate the excuse to stand close to Cameron? Violet tried to detect some signs of attraction. She enjoyed the possibility of a budding romance as much as most women.

That is, she enjoyed it until she realized how neat and tidy it *almost* was. Trevor and Alison were a couple. Logan and Audra were a couple. If Cameron and Katie started dating, Violet and Ryan would be the only single ones left. How long would it take for the others to start jokes about them getting together? How annoying would Ryan find that? Violet cringed at the thought of him telling everyone to stop kidding about something that would never happen.

"I think that's our cue to leave," Audra said. She was waving at Violet.

"Why?" Violet asked, though she should have said, "What is?" because she had completely missed whatever the cue had been.

"If they get the Tichu, the game might end this round so..." Audra glanced at Katie and communicated that they needed to get her out of there before the game ended.

Violet nodded. Logan was supposed to invite Cameron to lunch after the game, which Audra wouldn't want him to do in front of Katie. She wished Ryan luck and was pleased to see him acknowledge it with a quick smile. At least he noticed she was leaving.

2

Violet held up a weirdly folded piece of paper. Was it poor origami? If she used her imagination, it could be a star. Maybe. Why had she saved it?

There was a wooden chest in Violet's bedroom. She'd had it longer than she could remember, and it contained all the little keepsakes she'd collected through childhood. She hadn't looked through it since high school, and it'd probably been that long since she'd even opened it. She was digging through it now in the hopes of triggering a memory she could use for the speech she didn't want to write.

She wasn't getting anything from the sort of almost maybe a star thing. She dropped it into her trash pile. She hadn't found any inspiration, but at least she was making progress on cleaning out the chest.

Unfortunately, she was also making progress on getting stiff from sitting on the floor. Violet scooped up her trash pile – it took a few tries to balance all the odd shapes – and made a short trip that would also stretch her legs. Once she was away from the chest, she didn't feel like going back. She looked around the quiet apartment. Audra wasn't back from her big matchmaking lunch yet. It was too quiet. Violet picked up her phone, intending to plug it into her soundbar for some music. Rosie had texted only a few minutes earlier asking if Violet was available for a video call. The music could wait.

Violet's sister appeared on the screen with her cat's tail swishing across her face. She gently pushed the animal into a sitting position on her lap as she said, "He thinks I sat down just to pet him, but I guess I can do both. What's going on with you today?"

"I was just trying to work on the speech for your wedding actually."

Rosie's hand dropped off her cat as her eyes lit up. "Progress finally! How's it coming? But don't give me details, remember?"

"Uh… I think you missed the part where I said I was *trying* to work on it. Progress is a stretch."

"Well, there's still a few weeks. I know you'll think of something great."

"I was looking through old stuff for ideas," Violet said, "and I did find some interesting things."

Rosie nodded to show she wanted to hear about them while the cat arched its back to get under her hand again.

"Remember Dane?"

"The creepy sock puppet?" Rosie laughed. "Don't tell me you still have that."

"I sure do," Violet said. "It's in my chest right next to the long veil from my First Communion. Odd combination."

"Dane would be an odd combination with anything. Dad is insane."

Violet smiled at the assessment.

The cat gave up getting attention and leapt to the floor. Rosie got more serious as she leaned forward. She used both hands to tuck her hair behind her ears. They both had dark brown or black hair, depending on whom you asked. Rosie's was super straight like their dad's while Violet's was super curly like their mom's. "Okay. So I wanted to talk because I have some good news and some bad news. Which do you want first?"

"Let's start with the bad," Violet said. "Better to get it over with."

"There's been another change in the wedding plans, and I'm going to need your help with something."

Violet nodded. It couldn't be worse than the speech. "What is it?"

"This is what you'll think is the good news. Nate talked me into music."

"For the reception? Yay!" Violet tried to sound happy but not thrilled. She already told her sister she thought no music was a mistake. There was no reason to gloat. But she might have to thank her future brother-in-law next time she saw him.

Rosie smiled as though she could tell Violet was holding back. "I'm glad you're excited because like I said, this is where I need your help. We don't want to hire a DJ because, well, lots of reasons. Will you put together a playlist for us? Nate knows someone with some good speakers we can borrow. He said you can plug just about any device in, and it'll sound great."

Violet was still trying not to smile too big. A playlist would be so much easier and more fun to write than a speech.

"Don't make it all fast songs though," Rosie said. "I know you keep saying it should be a party, but... We don't want a conga line or anything silly. It should be about half slower songs. There will be lots of couples so we'll need couple songs. And that brings me to the other good news/bad news thing."

"Oh, there's more?" Violet was distracted thinking which of her favorite songs should go in the list. There wouldn't just be music, there would be music she got to choose. This was really good news.

"Now that there's going to be some dancing, we decided to do a traditional first dance thing," Rosie said. "Nate and I will start. Then the rest of the wedding party will join us. That includes you, but don't worry."

Rosie held up a finger to stop the worry before Violet knew what to worry about. That started the worry.

"I already talked to Mom. She's going to let you have Dad. He's fine with it, too."

"Uh… fine with what?" Violet asked.

"He'll dance with you instead of Mom when we have the wedding party dance."

"Isn't the mother of the bride part of the wedding party?"

"Well, yeah, kind of. It's better if Mom sits out though because people will be like, oh, she'd old. She just needs to rest for a bit or something."

"As opposed to what people will think if *I'm* sitting out," Violet said. She wanted Rosie to say exactly what she thought but not enough to ask.

"That's why I arranged everything with Dad," Rosie said. "Nothing to worry about."

This conversation gave Violet the queasy feeling that "don't worry" equated with "you're not pathetic," which no one ever said unless someone was a little pathetic. She tried to think if she was missing any details that didn't have anything to do with her being the only single person at the wedding because that probably wasn't even as true as it felt. "Where does the music fit into the schedule? I'm assuming it's after lunch."

"Right after the speeches," Rosie said. "During the mingling time, which should only be the last hour, but I thought we should have a little more music than that in case we get ahead of schedule."

Violet nodded at the confirmation that her speech hadn't been eliminated by the addition of music. She hadn't gotten her hopes up for that, but it was a nice idea.

"Oh, I have to go." Rosie was looking off to the side. "Talk more soon?"

Violet waved as her sister disappeared from the screen. She set the phone down. She no longer felt like listening to music. Nor did she want to go back to searching through old junk. She felt like sulking for a minute before she decided what to do next.

A key in the lock told her that Audra was back. That was sure to be a welcome distraction. Audra was beaming about something. She went into her bedroom already squirming out of her coat and reemerged a few seconds later without it. She plopped onto the sofa with one leg tucked so she was facing Violet. She was smiling broadly and intentionally created a dramatic pause before she announced, "I am a genius!"

"I take it lunch went well."

"They are so cute together," Audra said. "It's perfect."

"What did Katie say when she found out Cameron was coming? Did you tell her before he got there?"

"Those two!" Audra sighed while fighting an exasperated smile. "They already talked and knew we were setting them up. They played along just to tease me."

Violet laughed because her roommate's reaction was funny, but also because she was happy for Katie. "So she didn't mind being set up?"

"She didn't even *need* to be set up."

"Wait. If they didn't need you, how are you a genius?"

"Because I knew they'd be good together." Audra's smug attitude was amusing. It was clear she was only facetiously taking credit.

Violet's heart wasn't fully in her laughs though, and Audra sensed it. She dropped her smile and said, "Now what's going on with you? You seemed a little... off when I first came in."

"I just talked to my sister."

"Oh. Wedding plans. Is she carving out twenty minutes of total silence in case there's anyone who isn't bored?"

"No. It's actually mostly good news," Violet said. "She relented on the music and is even letting me choose the songs."

Audra smiled in surprise. "Then why aren't you excited and, like, already making a playlist or something?"

"While we were talking, she said she wants to start with a wedding party couples dance and that I'm going to dance with my dad. She didn't ask me what I thought about that or how I would feel if I didn't have a dance partner. She just assumed I couldn't find someone willing to dance with me and that I would look pathetic sitting out and arranged everything... talked to Mom and Dad about it before she even talked to me."

"I agree she should have gotten your take first," Audra said with a sympathetic expression.

And just like that, Violet felt her spirit lift. It wasn't a big deal. She only needed to vent her frustration at not having been consulted. "Yeah, well, it's Rosie's wedding. If she wants me to dance with Dad, I'll dance with Dad."

"But maybe you won't have to." Audra wiggled her eyebrows to suggest a clever idea forming.

That made Violet nervous.

"I hope you don't think I've forgotten my mission."

Violet shook her head as she got more nervous about where Audra's mind was headed.

"I didn't forget," Audra insisted. "I've just been biding my time for an opportunity to get you and Ryan some time together. This could be the perfect opportunity."

"I cannot ask Ryan to come to a wedding with me." Violet knew that wouldn't work because she'd definitely considered it. A lot. "Weddings have very romantic overtones. It would sound like I'm asking for a date unless I explicitly state I want to go as friends. And if there's even the slightest chance he might think about me as... I don't want to be the one to close that door. And if I ask, and he doesn't want to or it goes badly, it'll ruin... lots of things. I mean, he's your brother. He lives next door. There would be no avoiding him, and we'd both just be embarrassed all the time."

Audra appeared overly patient, as though she was simply waiting for Violet to finish so she could say what should be obvious. "This is why I'm going to get *Ryan* to ask *you*."

Violet winced. There was no way that was going to end well. It sounded like something that would require subtlety and finesse. Audra was a wonderful friend with a ton of wonderful qualities. Subtlety was not one of them. "How do you plan to do that?"

"I just need to plant the right ideas."

"Which are?"

She sucked in a big breath as she prepared to lay out her plan. "Ryan is a nice guy, right? I mean, that's why you like him. Don't tell me it's *one* of the reasons because I don't want to hear about... He's nice. So all I have to do is get him to realize that it would be *nice* if he offered to go to the wedding with you. I can explain how Rosie's giving you a hard time about going alone because, well, that's one way to interpret it. And I'll mention how your mom has to sit out the dance because of the odd number of guys to girls in the wedding party. I think he'll figure it out."

"It sounds like you want to make him pity me."

"No, it's not pity." Audra's eyes went to the ceiling as she seemed to take an awful long time thinking of a better word. "Compassion," she said finally. "I just need to make it sound like a problem he can fix. Guys like to fix things."

Violet thought that was actually a fair point. She saw a flaw though. "But what if he has the same problem I do in not wanting to sound too much like a date?" Or worse, what if he had no trouble clarifying that he was only going as a favor to a friend? Violet had to admit that even though it would hurt, if she had no reason to hope, it would be better in the long run to know to stop hoping.

Audra frowned. "Yeah. We need to think of a way to take the pressure off. If he has to go out of his way to ask or make a phone call specifically for that purpose..."

Though there was some relief at this plan going sideways,

Violet mostly found herself wishing Audra could think of a way to keep up her meddling.

"This should be possible," Audra said. She still sounded determined. "All we need is a way for it to casually come up where he can make a low-key offer. But he usually only sees you on Friday nights and in front of the group might not be entirely low pressure." Then the light bulb came on. "Dessert."

"Dessert?" Violet didn't understand how one word was the answer.

"Remember when you made brownies and took them to the guys? We split so that a few of us were in the kitchen and a few not. There were several conversations so you and Ryan could easily talk amongst yourselves."

"I'm skeptical that it would be that easy."

"You just serve Ryan last so you don't have anywhere to go after you set his down. Then you chat. It'll be perfectly natural for you to mention this big event coming up, and that gives Ryan his opening."

Violet was amused by Audra's optimism.

Audra sighed at the disbelieving laughter. "Do I have to spell out the whole conversation?"

"Yes, I think that will be entertaining."

"Fine. How far away is the wedding? It'll be four weeks on Friday, right?"

Violet nodded. That sounded right.

"Okay. You say something like, my sister's wedding is only four weeks away now. Ryan will nod that he's listening, and that will get him thinking about how he wants to help out. Then you'll ask if I told him there's going to be music now. Again, perfectly natural that you'll be mentioning that because it's something you're happy about. Ryan will nod again because I will have told him that. Then he'll say, very casually, that I also mentioned you'd need a dance partner and that if you couldn't find anyone else, he would be available. Then you tell him that's a very *nice* offer that you would be glad to accept because otherwise you'd probably end up making your mom sit out. See? He's helping you help your mom. There's no pity in that."

The plan was entertaining, mostly because it was far from foolproof. "You know it's not going to happen like that, right?"

"Maybe not exactly, but close enough. Then you guys will spend lots of time talking at the wedding and boom! Another wedding in the works."

Violet didn't want to burst the bubble but she was poking it anyway. "Well, in addition to the careful orchestration of getting six other people to happen to stand away from me and Ryan, the whole plan might not be right because I think Ryan might be off desserts."

"What? Why do you think that?"

"He's lost a fair amount of weight since the summer," Violet said. "He's gotta be doing something different."

Audra's eyes darted around the room as she processed the information. "I hadn't noticed anything different but now that you mention it... No, I saw him eat a cookie at work last week so he's not completely off desserts. We'll make something not as rich as brownies, just in case."

"Like what?"

"Hmm." Audra smiled. "Gingerbread men."

Violet laughed at the way she said it as though it was the only right answer. "It's not even Thanksgiving."

"Exactly. Trevor especially will try to be difficult about it, and that will set up a friendly debate about how there is nothing inherently Christmasy about cookies in the shape of little people. That will make the mood light for you and Ryan to have a very casual discussion that ends in happily ever after."

"Wow. You are totally hopeless, aren't you?"

"I'm hope*ful*," Audra said.

3

Ryan saw it as a sign that Ben was not completely hopeless. The kid had been working in the kitchen for several months and had been reminded countless times that his phone was covered in germs and shouldn't be touched while handling food. This was the first time he'd seen Ben reach for it, then stop himself in time to not have to wash his hands before he finished cutting the melon. Maybe there would be less nagging in the future.

It might be greedy to hope for that though. The job was already by far the best he'd had. When he looked around the January Café, it still looked like his grandparents' place, still felt like their place. He had never considered that he might one day take it over until they offered it to him. Now it was starting to feel like his place as well as theirs. That was weird but not bad.

He was wondering if he could say the same thing about the look on Audra's face. She'd just come into the kitchen, dropped a rag into a bucket of disinfectant, then began to stare at him with her eyebrows scrunched together.

"What?" he asked.

"Have you lost weight?"

"I'm down about twenty-five pounds since the summer."

"Hmm." She continued to stare as though the simple fact required more thought.

"What?" he asked again.

"Violet and I were going to bring a treat when we stop in to check on the Tichu tonight, but she's concerned you might not appreciate it if you're trying to avoid sweets."

Violet had noticed. There probably wasn't anything to read into that. She paid attention to everything. "I've been trying to take better care of myself but nothing drastic. I still like an occasional treat."

"Good."

"What are you guys making?"

"It's a surprise."

"What is it?"

"You know what surprise means," Audra said, glaring at him for trying to trip her up.

Ben was making noise with his cleanup, mostly running water, and Audra pushed her way through the door back to the dining room. Her eyes said she expected Ryan to follow. He wasn't doing anything else at the moment. It was the middle of the afternoon and the only customers were a few older women at a table near the front. They were chattering over drinks and didn't require much attention.

Audra went behind the counter and turned to face him. "Violet and I were talking about something else and… I'm thinking maybe you can help."

"Is there a problem?"

"Yes. Rosie relented on the no music for the reception."

"How is that a problem?" Ryan asked. Violet had been disappointed that there wouldn't be music. This sounded as though a problem had been solved.

"Well, the music is good except… Now Rosie is arranging a special dance. First, she and Nate will dance, then they're supposed to be joined by the groomsman, Nate's brother, and his wife. Then the bridesmaid, Violet, and then the groom's parents and finally the bride's parents. It's practically choreographed." Audra waved her hands over the counter as though she was positioning dancers as she talked. "She has this idea that it's going to be more of a performance than... I don't know. She just wants the whole wedding party on display. You see the problem now, right?"

Ryan saw that the problem was his sister was implying Violet needed a dance partner while looking at him. But he decided to let her spin her wheels a bit. "Not really, no."

"Violet can't dance by herself."

"Why not?"

Audra seemed shocked he didn't understand. "It'll be a slow couple song, and she'll be on display and stuff."

"Doesn't Violet like to dance?"

"Yes, of course she likes to dance, but you are completely missing the point. Violet is going to be by herself. Rosie's solution is to have Violet dance with their dad, which makes their mom by herself instead. Violet feels bad about leaving her out."

"Why doesn't Violet just volunteer to sit out instead?"

"She tried," Audra said. "Rosie thinks it's more important for the bridesmaid to be dancing."

Ryan only nodded.

Audra sighed loudly. "Don't you see how much easier it would be if there was another guy to balance things out?"

It was time to stop the act. Ryan was getting insulted that she hadn't figured out he was messing with her. "How dense do you think I am?" he asked.

"What?"

"Do you really think I don't know you're trying to suggest *I* can dance with Violet?"

Audra crumpled her top half facedown on the counter, then stood up again. "If you know that, why are you trying to make me work so hard to show you?"

"It's kind of fun to watch you try to be subtle."

She shook her head but stopped suddenly as her eyes brightened. "So you'll do it?"

"Of course not," he said. "It's a terrible idea."

"How can you say that? Violet is great."

Violet was great. That wasn't the problem. "It's a terrible idea because, one, I'm not going to invite myself to a wedding. And two, it's pretty obvious you're trying to play matchmaker again."

"What makes you think that?" Audra managed to inject a bit of surprise in her voice, but the guilty flicker in her eyes gave her away.

"You've been gloating all week about your part in getting Cameron and Katie together, which if I understand correctly wasn't much of a part, and I heard you telling Addie you hoped for more chances to play matchmaker so it'd be obvious even if you weren't all 'Violet will be all alone. If only you could help me think of a guy to go with her. Oh, wait. You're a guy.'"

At least Audra was a good sport. She was fighting a laugh at his mocking. "That's not what I said."

"Uh-huh?"

She turned towards the dining room a moment before she held up a finger. "Stay right there."

He watched her grab a pitcher of ice water to go check on their one active table. Most of the women seemed to be waving her away. They might be finishing up. Audra said something that made them smile before she moved away. She was a valuable employee. But the look of concentration on her face as she returned to the back suggested she had stepped away at least partly to give herself time to rephrase her argument. Ryan prepared to hear more about how she wasn't trying to fix him up with Violet.

"I know it sounds like I'm trying to fix you up with Violet," Audra said, still replacing the pitcher under the counter, "but she really isn't excited about going to the wedding alone. Besides the dancing, she'll be surrounded by couples and people asking when her turn will be. She'd like to have someone to talk to. You do know how to talk, and you like to dance so it would be *nice* if you offered to go with her, which is not the same as inviting yourself."

"I think it is."

Audra pretended she didn't hear him. "And if the two of you happen to get along really well and want to spend more time together later, I don't see how anyone would be upset by that."

"You might as well stop plotting because Violet is too smart to fall into your trap, too."

"It's not a trap. It's a good idea." Audra glanced to the side at the sound of the door opening. "You just think about it, and then you'll realize I'm right," she said, then moved away to welcome some entering customers.

Ryan didn't have to think about it to know she was wrong. He didn't have a lot of time to think about it anyway. The place got gradually busier, and he put the conversation out of his mind until the evening when he was playing Tichu with the guys. The first game went well, at least for him and Trevor. They won in seven rounds.

Logan was his partner for the second game. It was usually during the second game that the girls came to watch. That was when he remembered that Audra was trying to meddle. Mostly, it made him wonder what she'd said to Violet. Would Violet be on guard against attempts to play along? Ryan hated the idea that Violet might be uncomfortable now that Audra was trying to push them together.

"Wait a minute," Trevor said. "I only have thirteen cards."

"I have fourteen," Ryan said.

Logan counted his aloud. Everyone else seemed to have the right number.

"They're probably just sticking," Ryan said. "We should have used the red one." They had two Tichu decks. The green one had been originally put aside to stay nice, but they started using it once the red one was worn and used it so long the red one was now better.

Trevor wrongly insisted that wasn't true, but he was too busy recounting his cards – and making sure none were stuck together –

24

to argue that the green cards didn't stick together.

Cameron looked under the table. "It's not on the floor."

The suggestion of the floor caused Ryan to examine it even though there was also a suggestion that the card wasn't there. Logan peered under the table, too.

"Oh," Trevor said. He sounded as though he was kicking himself. "It was in my lap."

The game resumed without anyone else kicking him for the delay. After a moment, Logan's phone – which was sitting on the table to record the score – lit up, and he said, "They're on the way."

Audra had been sending something like a countdown to when she and the others were coming with a mystery treat. She seemed to be trying to get them to guess. None of the guys were interested in playing that game. Mostly because they weren't all that picky about treats. There wasn't much they wouldn't eat. Ryan didn't want to play because every mention made him think that Violet had noticed he might not want a treat, and he really shouldn't be thinking about Violet at all. Now he was thinking she was on her way.

Ryan had an excellent hand though. He only needed to focus for a few minutes to play all his cards. Cameron was setting his final cards on the table when the doorbell rang.

It was mildly surprising that Violet was the first to enter because Audra always led the way. Violet said, "Hi," and smiled at Ryan, but she smiled at the other guys, too. Audra was right behind her, followed by Katie and Alison. All four of them had a small plate in each hand. Ryan briefly wondered how Audra had managed to ring the doorbell and let herself in with her hands full. Maybe that had something to do with why she hadn't been first inside. Violet had helped somehow.

Looking back at Violet, Ryan noticed that she was holding the plates unnaturally high, near her shoulders. She glanced at Audra, in a way that said she was humoring her. Apparently, Audra wanted everyone to hold the dessert high enough that the guys still sitting couldn't see it. She was working awfully hard for buildup on something that would likely be eaten in two minutes.

"Oh, they're almost done," Audra announced. She had moved far enough into the room to be behind Logan. Her face confirmed they were almost done because of the depressing state of what he was holding. Trevor went out almost immediately, and he stood up as soon as the points were counted.

He wanted to greet Alison more fully than just a wave. As soon as he saw what she was holding, he said, "Gingerbread men? Audra, it's way too early for Christmas."

"I knew you'd say that," she said. "And gingerbread men are not necessarily Christmasy. Notice how I didn't use any red or green frosting?"

A plate appeared on the table in front of Ryan. The cookie had mostly white frosting with a blue scarf and boots and brown eyes and hair. Some time had gone into the treat. He turned back long enough to thank Violet. She only mouthed, "You're welcome," before putting her eyes back on the expected debate.

"Just because some people associate gingerbread with Christmas doesn't make it inherently Christmasy," Audra said.

"*Most* people," Trevor corrected.

"It kind of does," Logan said. "Jingle Bells doesn't actually mention Christmas anywhere in the lyrics. But if I started singing it, you'd be thinking Christmas because people have made it a Christmas song."

"That's not what we'd think if you started singing," Ryan said. Logan was next door to tone-deaf.

He caught the jab with a smile before he bit his cookie's head off.

"Well, they are good even if it's the wrong season," Trevor admitted. He was moving into the kitchen to talk to Alison, and evidently wanted Audra to know she hadn't won anything just because he wasn't going to continue the argument.

Ryan picked up his cookie, but before he could enjoy a taste, he realized that Audra had won something. She'd told him she would give him an opportunity to talk to Violet, whether he wanted it or not, and she'd gotten everyone to go along with her plans. Katie had pulled Cameron to another corner of the room, and Audra made sure Logan turned away from the table to talk to her. Violet was left alone somewhere behind Ryan. Sitting there eating his cookie with his back to her while the others engaged in semi-private conversations felt rude. Ryan swallowed while he turned his chair to face Violet.

"Did you and Audra make these together?" he asked.

"Sort of." She was tracing her cookie with her finger rather than picking it up to eat it. "I baked them while she was still at work. Then she decorated them while we were playing Tichu."

"*While* you were playing?"

"Yeah. She jumped up to work on them between rounds or if the game slowed because we were talking."

That sounded annoying to Ryan. He could easily picture having to call Audra back to the table every time it was her turn. But he just nodded. Violet seemed entertained by it. Her eyes smiled as she spoke, and her hair bounced a little. She kept her dark hair piled near the top of her head with some loose curls hanging down. Lately, whenever Ryan looked at it, he pictured wrapping one of those curls around his finger. It looked as though it'd be a perfect fit.

"Anyway," Violet continued, "the frosting didn't have time to set, at least on most of them, and that's why we had to bring them over on separate plates."

Ryan was glad he was chewing. It saved him from having any immediate reaction to the disappointing statement. He'd been wondering if there was any chance Violet was cooperating with Audra's plan to divide the room into pairs. Now he wondered if the others had somehow arranged it behind her back or if she explained it away because it embarrassed her. Did she know about Audra's other matchmaking plans? "Audra told me your sister decided to have music at the reception after all," he said.

"Did she tell you I get to pick it out?" Violet smiled brightly. He nodded.

"I already made the whole playlist, which is good and bad."

"How so?" Was this where she mentioned the number of slow songs, where she'd be missing a partner?

"Well, it was fun, and since it was also for the wedding, I felt fully justified in putting off the speech-writing." Her expression shifted with the bad news. "But it was so fun I finished in like two days. So now I have no excuse not to work on the impossible speech."

"Have you had any ideas?" Violet really seemed to be struggling with the speech, and Ryan wanted to help. But since he'd never even met her sister, all he could do was try to sound sympathetic.

"I, um… I thought of a possible ending, and…" Violet spun her cookie around on her plate as she stalled. She still hadn't taken a bite. "Would you give me an honest opinion on whether or not it's a good idea?" Her eyes lifted to meet his as she made the request.

He couldn't refuse when she looked at him like that, all plaintive and beautiful. But agreeing to honesty on something he hadn't heard yet was dangerous. He braced himself.

"I was thinking," Violet began slowly, "that since she asked me to include memories that it might be funny if I say something about how this one time she asked me to write a speech and I couldn't live up to the expectations but she forgave me and how forgiveness is important in marriage."

Ryan breathed a sigh of relief. "That's great," he said. "Really. It's serious because forgiveness is important in any relationship but also… I think people will smile at the memory of right now."

Violet bit the side of her lip, looking unconvinced. "The reason I'm worried… um, I need to make sure it doesn't sound like I'm making fun of her. Rosie went to a friend's wedding a few months ago, and the best man gave a speech that just completely roasted both the bride and the groom. Some people thought it was funny, but Rosie thought it was kind of mean and could tell that her friend was upset by it, and... even though I do think she's asking *a lot* from this speech, I still don't want to hurt her feelings. Especially on what should be a happy day."

"I don't think it would," Ryan said. "I mean, I don't know your sister, and it might depend on exactly how you word it, but I think if it sounds like you're making fun of anyone, you're making fun of yourself for not... being a great orator. So many people hate public speaking that they'll sympathize without judging Rosie at all."

"Hmm." Her lips pressed against a smile. "Not a great orator? Nice random use of a ten-dollar word."

"What?" He tried to look surprised and not as though he'd been trying to impress anyone. "That's just part of my naturally expansive vocabulary."

The comment earned him a laugh. "Thank you," Violet said. "I think you might be right."

Ryan ate the last of his cookie without saying anything about being right about his vocabulary. He knew that wasn't what she meant, and he'd already gotten one laugh. Another joke would probably be trying too hard. Besides, he'd realized that almost everyone else had finished the desserts. Trevor was already back at the table, and Audra had moved close enough that she might be trying to overhear how her plan was working out. When Ryan turned back to the game, the other guys took their seats, too. Audra and Violet collected the plates while Logan dealt, then all the girls left with Alison.

"It was my deal, wasn't it?" Logan asked.

Cameron shrugged.

Trevor nodded.

Ryan was too distracted to care. He was annoyed because he found himself wishing his sister was a better matchmaker.

Obviously, she was wrong. Violet had a perfect opportunity to mention that she didn't want to go to the wedding alone. She said nothing about it. She'd asked his opinion, seemed to care what he thought about her speech. But she steered clear of anything that might even hint she wanted someone to go to a wedding or dance with her, no hints of being open to romantic interest. Audra was wrong. Her scheming wouldn't lead to anything other than a repeat of past failures. Violet was another woman who didn't want more than friendship from him.

4

Violet didn't know what she was up to, but Audra was definitely up to something. After last week's Tichu game, she'd grilled Violet about her conversation with Ryan. Audra had been delighted to find out that he'd been the one to bring up the music, that he'd actually done his part. She was equally *un*delighted to learn that Violet had not followed the script that had been laid out for her. But Violet wasn't convinced that Ryan had been playing any kind of part. He'd simply been trying to have a friendly chat with the only person left after Audra got everyone else to turn their backs on him. And Violet couldn't talk about dancing, probably couldn't even think about dancing with Ryan, without turning a few shades of red. That would have zapped the casual out of the conversation. After expressing a little frustration, Audra assured Violet that she would continue to work on the situation.

The assurance left Violet unsure how to feel. Was Audra going to come through with a brilliant plan or would her meddling annoy any glimmer of interest right out of Ryan? They hadn't talked about him the rest of the week so Violet tried to put it out of her mind. She would simply try to make the most of the time she'd see him when they popped in on the guys' game. Ryan never seemed to mind the interruption. He was more even-tempered than Trevor, and his lack of irritation was probably nothing more than a lack of irritation. But Violet couldn't stop herself from wishing he was happy to see her.

She got home from work a few minutes after five and immediately put on some music to dive into a workout. She imagined it would be a good stress reliever if she had a stressful job. She didn't. She was a receptionist at a dance studio. Her primary duties were checking the kids in and out to note attendance and answering a ton of phone calls and emails about the schedule. She also created some occasional reports or updated some bookkeeping, whatever the manager asked. The atmosphere was rarely frazzled.

Violet's exercise didn't relieve stress as much as prevent it. She listened to Christian rock. The lyrics sometimes inspired praise or gratitude for the blessings in her life. Mostly, she found the rhythm of the songs, combined with the rhythm of her movements, to be meditative. She could let her body move while her mind asked God what they needed to talk about that day.

Ryan had been the subject often over the last year. At first, she wondered if she was being impatient, if she wanted a romantic relationship with Ryan because she wanted a romantic relationship and he was one of the only single guys she knew. Cameron helped her put those fears to rest. He was dating Katie now, but he'd been single most of the time she'd known him and couldn't remember any thoughts of him being a possible backup. That seemed to prove that Violet's feelings for Ryan were based on Ryan and not a generic desire for love.

Of course, once she had diagnosed herself as legitimately smitten, Violet's conversations with God began to revolve around whether or not she had any reason to hope he might feel the same about her. She wanted some sort of sign, and she wanted it to be clear, and she wanted it to say there *was* reason for hope. That left her in danger of ignoring evidence to the contrary. She tried to pray for peace regardless, but she knew she wasn't spending enough time on the possibility of disappointment.

Violet had a quick and easy dinner after a good workout, then a very warm shower. Most nights, this routine had her in pajamas by

7 PM, around the time Audra got home. But on Fridays, Violet found something comfortable but still appropriate for playing Tichu with friends. There was a knock as Violet was pulling a fuzzy sweater over her head. She must have spent more time in the shower than she thought. Violet rushed to answer the door still straightening her sweater.

"Hey, Violet." It was Alison. She rushed inside hugging her coat closed.

"Hi," Violet said. "You have a good week?"

"Pretty good. Did Audra tell you the plan for tonight?"

This was Violet's first hint that Audra was up to something. "Is the plan different than usual?"

Alison smiled somewhat mysteriously. "I'm sure we'll have fun."

There was another knock before Violet could ask any questions. She wasn't surprised to find Katie since Audra used her key. "Oh, you look cold," Violet said, gesturing her inside. Katie also had her arms wrapped around herself. It was well below freezing, but still no snow on the ground or in the forecast.

"Hi." Katie looked past Violet to include Alison in her greeting, then brought her eyes back. "Did Audra tell you the plan for tonight?"

This was the second clue that Audra was up to something. "Apparently not," Violet said. "What is the plan?"

Katie and Alison looked at each other as though they didn't know who was supposed to tell Violet what. Fortunately, a key in the lock signaled the arrival of the evening's conductor. The other ladies appeared relieved by the sound.

"Hi, everyone! Sorry I'm late," Audra said. "I stayed to help Ryan close so he could get home and be surprised. He's a couple minutes behind me still. Just a second." She came in, walked past the others and disappeared into her bedroom, talking the whole way.

The part of the speech that caught Violet's attention was that

Ryan would be surprised by something. Was that part of the secret plan? She turned curious eyes on Katie, and then Alison. Both of them only smiled in response.

Audra returned having dropped her bag but still wearing a coat. Violet realized the other women had made no move to shed theirs either. And Audra was walking right back towards the door. "Come on," she said. "I talked to Logan, and you talked to Cameron, right?"

"Yeah," Katie said, laughing. "He's waiting in his car for me to text him that Trevor's on board."

Audra looked as though she was going to roll her eyes but stopped. "Actually, it'll be easier for us to outnumber him this way." She held the door open for the others, then nodded encouragingly to Violet.

It seemed that Violet was at least included in the plan she knew nothing about. She grabbed a jacket and a hat to put over her wet hair before hurrying to the door.

Audra stopped her at the threshold long enough to lean in and whisper, "Don't worry. Everyone thinks this is totally my idea."

Violet nodded. Whatever this was, she doubted anyone wouldn't see Audra's name all over it. But she understood Audra was saying the others had helped her orchestrate some time with Ryan without telling them it was something Violet wanted.

When they entered Trevor and Ryan's apartment, only Trevor and Logan were sitting at the table. Violet should have had enough clues to expect that, but she was still feeling a step behind. She wasn't the only one. As she came in, she heard Trevor ask Audra what she was doing there.

"Well, hello to you, too," she answered sarcastically.

"You guys plan to watch the whole game today?"

"I'm here to propose a change of plans," Audra said. "We should switch up the teams." She grinned in anticipation of a positive reaction.

Trevor turned a wary eye to Logan. "This is why you asked me to remember something would be a one-time suggestion."

Logan calmly shuffled the cards in front of him without saying anything.

Audra didn't give him a chance anyway. "Oh, yes, just for tonight," she said. "I'm not messing with your guy time... too much. Just for tonight, I'll leave Katie and Alison here and take Logan and Ryan back to our place."

The sound of cards shuffling filled the silence while Trevor processed the idea. Violet liked the sound of the temporary arrangement.

"It's not a terrible idea," Trevor said. "I just don't like the part where I'm ambushed by it. Oh, wait a minute." He gestured to the empty chairs. "Is this why everyone is late? So you could outvote me?"

"Cameron's on his way," Katie volunteered, still putting her phone away.

"Ryan really had some work to do," Audra said. "He doesn't know anything about this yet."

"I'm sure he'll be thrilled," Trevor mumbled. He still had his eye on Katie. He seemed to realize that she'd been in contact with Cameron as part of some sort of divide and conquer approach, and he did not approve.

Violet thought that, so far at least, it was kind of brilliant. She was reserving final judgement until she saw Ryan's reaction.

Cameron came in, and Logan gave up his seat for Alison, which meant all the players for one game were assembled. Trevor appeared happier with the plan when it meant he could start. Audra wished them all luck and motioned for Violet and Logan to follow her.

Where was Ryan? If he arrived after they left, Trevor would explain the situation. Ryan would be fine with it. He'd be happy they were still playing. But Violet wanted to see the moment he found out. She wanted to see if there was anything unguarded in that moment, something that said he might enjoy some extra time with Violet or was annoyed with Audra for trying to push them together. Well, in all honesty, she only wanted to see the reaction if it was good news. But she needed to see it if it wasn't.

The guys' entrance was on the side of the house. Violet followed Audra and Logan towards the front where they met Ryan.

"Come on, man." Logan stopped him from going to his own door. "We've been summoned over here tonight."

Ryan came inside with the others with no comment or reaction at all. It appeared he just wanted to get where it was warm before he figured out what was happening. As soon as the door was closed, he turned to Logan and asked if he'd seen the previous night's hockey game.

Logan nodded and began to recount a power play goal. Violet took advantage of being unnoticed to ditch her coat and hat. She gathered her damp and now very cold curls and loosely clipped it all to the top of her head. She tried to tell by feel whether the spirals draped okay or if she'd left any sticking up. It was probably fine. Ryan glanced her direction, still talking about hockey penalties.

Audra had taken the Tichu cards off the shelf. Violet rushed over and asked under her breath if she'd done her hair right. That seemed less obvious than rushing off to a mirror. Audra assured her that it looked good, then held up the cards to address the guys. "Throw your coats on the couch if you want, then join us at the table."

There was a blue polo shirt under Ryan's coat. It was Violet's favorite. The color matched his eyes, eyes she was trying to catch for hints of his opinion of the situation. Audra would probably have some intricate reasoning for why he should or shouldn't be on her team, sitting next to or across from her, but she wondered which Ryan would prefer. And what would that mean? He turned around the same time as Logan, and they were both looking past her.

Logan smirked at Ryan before moving towards the table. Violet saw that Audra had been gesturing Logan to a specific seat behind her, which made the situation feel more contrived than if she had simply asked him to be her partner. Violet tried to ignore her heating face. Maybe Ryan would think the pink was from being outside.

He smiled at her and made a joke of it. "Looks like the lovebirds want to lose to us as some sort of bonding experience."

She returned the smile naturally because that was funny.

"Hey," Logan said. "No trash talking. This is a friendly game."

"It's not trash talk." Ryan claimed the chair next to Logan and across from Violet. "I'm just being honest about the fact that Violet is good."

A few degrees of color added to Violet's face at the comment, even though it wasn't a serious compliment. She watched Audra deal the cards. Focusing on her friend helped her relax. "Anything interesting at work today?"

"Well, my boss is still as mean as ever." Audra shot Ryan a wicked grin.

He calmly replied that he wouldn't have to be so mean if she wasn't so incompetent.

The playful exchange made Violet smile. Audra had been concerned that working for her brother might get tense, but they seemed to have gotten closer than ever.

"How was your week, Violet?" Ryan asked. "I hope the kids are still cute?"

"Of course they are. Things were a tad hectic this week as we just ordered the costumes for the Christmas show and then had several parents change their minds about whether or not their kids were coming."

"And how does that make more work for you?" Ryan had been dealt a full hand but hadn't picked it up yet. His interest seemed genuine and not merely an effort to be polite.

Violet still tried to keep her answer somewhat concise. No point testing his enthusiasm by delaying the game. "We try to let everyone participate even if they join late, and to refund costume fees if anyone drops out. But we don't have the budget to buy a bunch of extra, just-in-case costumes. So I'm constantly going back to my spreadsheet of measurements to see who might be able to go up or down a size to shift a costume we have to one we need. Everything worked out last year, but I think at least one family is going to be disappointed this year."

"I suppose it doesn't help to point out that none of the people who committed by the deadline will be disappointed."

"I'm sure it wouldn't help to say that to anyone, but I plan to be thinking it if I have to say, 'Sorry, your kid can't perform' because it will make me feel less guilty." Violet picked up her cards, which seemed to signal Ryan to do the same.

The first few rounds were fun. Violet and Ryan took an early lead, and he commented that the bomb she was dealt was proof of her excellent skills. Violet's favorite part was the different perspective she got when she was facing Ryan rather than watching from behind. She had never appreciated the way he silently communicated with his partner. It wasn't anything that gave away hints or advice. There was a quick nod when she took a trick or widened eyes when someone on the other team played something impressive. Without a word, he repeatedly said he was on her side.

Ryan was shuffling for a new round the next time anyone said anything not related to the game. "I kind of want to ask how your speech is coming, Violet, but I don't want to add any pressure if it isn't going well." He began to deal slowly to give her time to answer.

"I have thought of a few stories I might use," Violet said. "But I might have to give up on making them entertaining. I worry so much about sounding like I'm making fun of Rosie that anything I write comes out bland and... not entertaining."

"At least you have some ideas," Ryan said. "You sound more optimistic than you did before."

Violet felt more optimistic. She'd thought picking out stories would be the hardest part and now hoped she'd get the wording right eventually. She picked up the first half of her cards to avoid looking too happy that Ryan had picked up on her mood shift.

Violet's leg jerked in response to a kick from Audra. She glanced at the guys to see if either had noticed. Logan appeared pretty focused on his cards and Ryan on passing out the last few of them. Then she turned to see what Audra wanted. Her blonde hair was pulled forward over one shoulder, presumably to prevent Ryan from seeing what her eyes were doing. But since she usually kept her hair back, it was more likely to draw attention. Violet looked back at her cards. Hopefully, Audra wouldn't make any more weird expressions if she knew Violet wasn't watching them.

Did she really expect Violet to say something about not wanting to go to the wedding alone right now? Hey, Ryan, want to come with me so you can watch the speech I just said will be incredibly boring? Or did Audra want her to continue the conversation in general? Even that would be awkward now that Violet was wondering if Ryan asked about the speech in the first place because Audra had kicked him.

Ryan set down his cards to pass. "Do you think we should let them catch up a little now or just keep racking up points?"

Violet smiled at the jokey question.

Logan said, "*When* we start to catch up, it won't be because anyone let us."

"Definitely not," Audra agreed. "But I do think they make a good team." She wiggled her eyebrows meaningfully.

Violet cringed. She didn't want to know what Ryan thought of that implication, but she couldn't help herself from taking a peek. His eyes flickered up to hers, then back to his cards. Twice. Was it possible he wanted to gauge her thoughts on the matter? And was that even a good thing? Maybe he only wanted to be sure she wasn't getting any ideas from Audra's hopes. Something about the glances was encouraging though. Violet tried to think of something clever to say about their big lead.

And then the doorbell rang. She glanced at Audra, who confirmed with her expression that she wasn't expecting anyone either. "I'll get it," Violet said.

There was a hint of déjà vu when she found Alison standing there hugging herself against the cold. Violet instinctively waved her inside. Everyone else looked up with obvious surprise to see Alison return. Tension exploded in the few seconds she didn't say anything. Violet felt especially overwhelmed as it seemed wrong to return to her seat until they knew why Alison had left the other game.

"Um…" Alison fiddled with the zipper on her coat, then adopted a confident air. "I think Katie and Cameron would appreciate it if someone helped them finish the game."

Violet immediately turned to Audra to see her reaction. Her eyes said that she also heard which name Alison didn't say and suspected the same reason for the tension.

Ryan stood and motioned Alison towards his seat. "Sure, yeah… uh, you can play for me and I'll see… what I can do over there." He added a quiet, "Goodnight," as he walked past Violet to the exit.

There were a few seconds of complete silence when the door closed behind him. Then Alison took a step towards the table and Violet followed.

Neither had quite sat down when Logan made a move to stand. "Maybe I should go, too. If Ryan's not here," he paused to glance a little too significantly at Violet, "then you don't really need me to…" He trailed off, waiting for Audra's instructions.

"No," she said. "Or maybe. I think… Katie was excited to play with Cameron." Audra looked at Alison for confirmation while trying not to look at Alison.

"She's having fun."

It might have been her imagination, but Violet thought she heard some added inflection on the word she. After Logan's notable glance, she sunk into her chair. Violet had nothing to do with this plan, didn't even know about it until it happened. But as she watched it fall apart, she couldn't help wondering how many people were thinking it was her fault.

Audra's face wrestled with indecision and Logan still had a hand on the table, waiting to see if he should push himself up or not.

"You should stay," Audra said finally. "But maybe if… Let's just play."

Logan relaxed and reached for the deck.

"No," Audra said.

He sighed and started to stand.

"No, I mean," she waved for him to sit back down, "it's not your deal. It's mine."

"Oh. Right."

Audra took the cards and began to quietly pass them out. The mood did improve when they had a game to distract them. It remained subdued though. Alison left as soon as they were finished, sounding friendly but having never taken off her coat. Violet said goodnight and ducked into her bedroom to give Audra a moment to say goodbye to Logan without having to step out into the cold for privacy.

There was a prayer journal on her nightstand next to the book she was reading. She'd gotten it a few years ago because Audra used one, and it seemed like a good idea. Violet had never written in hers. Still, the pretty cover served as a good reminder to say some prayers before she picked up the book. The disastrous night was probably the end of Audra's matchmaking efforts. Violet didn't know what to pray about that. Audra really didn't seem cut out for matchmaking, and yet Violet was getting nowhere with Ryan on her own. She clearly needed help. Mostly, she prayed that this wasn't also the end of Alison and Trevor's relationship.

5

He didn't want to ask, but he did want to know what Audra
wanted. Ryan had been counting up orders for Thanksgiving pies.
When he looked up, he found Audra standing in front of him. She
seemed to expect something.

"Do you want to know how many?"

"I'm sure it's a lot," she said.

"It's already about the same as last year, and we might get some
more orders tomorrow."

Audra nodded but seemed far from satisfied.

"What?" he said.

"What's your plan?"

"My plan?"

"For making the pies."

"This might be my first year in charge, but we've all helped
with the Thanksgiving pies since we were kids," Ryan said. "I think
I have a pretty good handle on the plan."

Audra rolled her eyes as though he wasn't understanding her
question. "*Who* is going to make the pies?"

Quite a few people in town got their Thanksgiving pies from
the January Café. They would be picked up on Wednesday so most
of the pies were made on Tuesday. An extra employee would help
during the day, and a few friends and family members would come
in after hours when the ovens weren't needed for anything else.

Audra could read the work schedule and talk to their friends and family. Ryan was sure she knew exactly who would be making pies so he really wasn't understanding her question. "You know who."

"Logan and Trevor are going to help, right?"

"Yes."

"And?"

She wanted the whole list spelled out for some reason. He played along. "Well, Mom and Dad are staying home this year because they think we have enough help. Katie said she would like to help so of course Cameron is in. And Trevor and Logan and Violet. Grandma is coming, but she's not going to help. She said she wants to watch the next generation taking up the mantle of tradition... or something."

Audra appeared to be suppressing a laugh. She had heard their grandma's overly sentimental speech on the subject, too. But then she said, "So you asked her?"

"Asked her about what?" Ryan had not asked Grandma May why she was being dramatic about pies.

"If she'd come help."

They both knew she was coming and not helping. Something was still fishy about the whole conversation. "What are you talking about?"

"Violet."

Of course. Ryan should have guessed it had something to do with Violet. Audra hadn't brought her up for a few days so she was due to try to interfere again. But he still didn't know what Audra thought he should have done.

Audra sighed at his confusion. "Did you ask Violet if she'd come Tuesday night to help us with pies?"

"Didn't you ask her?"

"You were supposed to ask her on Friday."

"I was?"

"I know you didn't get a chance during the game like I planned because it... went a little off the rails." She paused to acknowledge the awkward memory before plowing ahead. "But I know you could have found another opportunity. You have her number."

"But you live with her," Ryan said. "Why would you assume I would be the one to ask her?"

"That should be obvious."

It was obvious from the wiggling eyebrows that Audra believed asking Violet to help with this work-related task – a task she'd already helped with the last two years – would suddenly cause her to have romantic interest in Ryan. It was also obvious that his sister was delusional. There was no point in trying to reason with an unreasonable person. Plus, he did want Violet to help. "Fine. I'll text her about the pies."

Audra walked away smiling victoriously.

Ryan sat at his desk to ask Violet if she'd be willing to help and apologized for the request coming at the last minute. He didn't blame Audra. Violet was smart enough to figure out for herself that the person who lived with her should be blamed for no one asking sooner. He didn't know if he'd get a reply right away. He waited a minute for one anyway. He liked thinking about Violet being happy to hear from him. He liked thinking about Violet in general. Except that he knew he shouldn't. He'd been down this road before.

A good romantic relationship should start with a solid friendship and build from there. Ryan had gotten the friendship part several times. But when he'd suggested a romantic turn, all the women had said they preferred to stay friends. Then, as soon as they realized it was weird to try to be friends after he'd expressed interest in more, they stopped spending time with him altogether. Maybe that meant the friendships hadn't been that solid. But if something like that happened with Violet, it might affect his relationship with his sister. And with some of their mutual friends as well. All of those relationships were more important than any he'd risked before.

It was better not to ride Audra's fantasy train. Ryan stuffed his phone in his pocket as he returned to the kitchen. He intended to concentrate on work. Unfortunately, it was late afternoon and pretty quiet in the restaurant. Dinner prep seemed to be well in hand and nothing was calling his attention aside from Audra's ridiculously satisfied smile.

Ryan found something to clean so he could ignore Audra. She chose not to ignore him. After only a minute, she came up and asked what Violet had said.

"Nothing yet," he said.

She grinned and twisted her shoulders in a brief dance.

That was just too irritating to ignore. "I asked her to help make pies," he said. "Don't smile like it's a big deal when it's not a big deal."

"It's the beginning of a big deal," Audra said. "I predict you two will be officially a couple by Christmas."

"I predict you will have Violet seriously ticked off by Christmas if you keep making those predictions."

"But not you?" She widened her eyes at the inferred hopes.

"I'm *already* annoyed with you."

She smiled as though she didn't believe him, which was very annoying. Worse was that the slicer wasn't fully clean so he couldn't remove himself from the conversation.

"I'll tell you how it's going to happen." Audra waved a hand as she set the scene in her imagination. "Violet is right now happy to find out you were thinking about her coming to make pies tomorrow. That will have her slightly mushy while she's here. I haven't figured it out yet, but somehow we'll get the two of you working close to each other but not too close to anyone else so you can talk. Your job will be to make sure you bring up her sister's wedding."

"My job will be to make pies."

Audra continued with no hint she'd heard the interruption. "Once you're on the subject of the wedding, she's bound to mention

46

something about dancing or being alone or something that will give you the opportunity to *finally* tell her you'd be willing to accompany her. And if you're at a wedding together… I mean, weddings are like the personification of romance. Or no, that's not the right word. It's not a person, but… Weddings are the embodiment of romance, and… Wait. Is that the same thing?"

Ryan was actually kind of amused by his sister's nonsensical speech to herself. She was just so intense, as though getting the explanation right mattered.

"Anyway," she shook her head, "the point is that very few things are more romantic than weddings so there's no way things won't snowball from there. Tell me that's not the perfect plan."

"That's not the perfect plan."

She fought a laugh before straightening her face. "I mean, seriously, what holes can you possibly poke in my setup?"

"Well, right off the bat, there is no way Violet is in any way flattered to be asked at the last minute to be an unpaid volunteer."

"Oh, she totally is. Or she will be whenever she gets the message. I talked to her about making pies at least a week ago so I know she wants to help. She'll know the only reason you wanted to confirm is because you were thinking about her being here."

"The only reason I wanted to confirm," he stressed her incorrect word, "is because you told me you didn't ask her."

Audra held up a finger. "I said you needed to ask."

"Because you didn't."

"That's not the same thing," she said.

That was something they could agree on. Ryan did not enjoy feeling tricked, but he said nothing about it. Audra was more likely to gloat than apologize. He certainly wasn't going to tell Violet that he was sorry he asked her unnecessarily. Because he wasn't. He was glad he was expecting a response from her. Not that he was going to say that either. Lucky for both of them, Audra didn't stick around. She went to check on customers in the dining room.

Violet texted a few hours later that she was looking forward to helping, and that she could almost smell the pies baking already. It was a lovely image, Violet with her eyes closed in contentment as she inhaled the aroma. It was a lovely image that was going to get Ryan in trouble. Audra already suspected he wasn't pushing back against her matchmaking schemes. As soon as Violet figured that out, well, he hoped at least Tichu night could survive it.

****

The January Café was generally busier during lunch. Katie was among the regulars and Cameron joined her more often than not. On Tuesday, they came in for dinner instead so they could linger afterwards until it was time to make the pies. Trevor and Logan came in as they finished eating and piled into the same booth. Violet joined them only a few minutes later. By the time Ryan said goodnight to the last employee and came out to get his evening crew, Audra was standing at the end of the table with Grandma May. They were all laughing, enjoying each other's company. Ryan could see plainly what was at stake if he made an unwelcome move towards Violet.

Grandma May saluted when she saw him coming. "Seven of us reporting for pie duty, sir."

Ryan smiled with everyone else, more at her infectious cheerfulness than her quip. He gestured back towards the kitchen. "All right. Let's do this."

Three workstations were already cluttered with the tools and ingredients Ryan had been setting up as the shift ended. His after-hours crew mostly remained huddled by the door waiting to be told what to do. He asked if anyone had preferences on assignments and saw plenty of heads shaking in response.

Then Cameron spoke up. "Full disclosure, I know almost nothing about making pies. Whatever you have me do, I'll need detailed instructions. Seriously, talk to me like I'm an idiot because when it comes to cooking, I am an idiot."

Grandma May squealed and rushed over to him. "Oh! I love teaching people how to cook," she said. "I was only going to watch, but I can't pass on an opportunity to share some wisdom. You and, uh... what's your name again?"

"Katie."

"That's right. You and Katie are with me. We'll be the pumpkin pie team. Assuming that's okay with the boss." Grandma May sent Ryan a look asking for permission to move ahead.

He was momentarily stunned that the woman who made the recipes they were about to use – and who was clearly the boss with a capital B – might actually defer to him on anything. Then he simply nodded and said, "That sounds great."

"It's perfect," Audra said. "It makes sense to have three people on the apple pies since they take the most work so Trevor can help me and Logan with those. If that's okay with the boss." The look she sent didn't convey asking for permission so much as daring him to think of a good reason to argue.

Ryan didn't have one. He nodded again.

"I guess that leaves us with pecan," Violet said.

And then Ryan began to wonder exactly how convenient that was. Surely Audra had pulled Trevor onto her team on purpose. But had Grandma May known to give her that chance? And had Cameron said something about his dismal cooking skills intentionally to get Grandma off the sidelines? None of that would really matter unless Violet suspected they were all conspiring against her. He might have to apologize for everyone being stupid. He didn't want to hear her agree that was what they were to think she'd fall for him.

Her expression was a mix of amusement and forced patience. What she suspected was that Ryan was staring into space.

"Pecan. Right," he said. "I remember you were good at crust last year. Do you want to start on that while I grab some eggs from the cooler?"

"Sure."

Music started playing while he was gone. Audra had it by her team. Ryan guessed – mostly by the wink she directed his way – that she was creating background noise to keep the separate conversations private. It was unnecessary but not hurting anything.

He began to mix up some filling near Violet. "Did Alison help you secure the win after I left on Friday?"

"Uh... yeah. It wasn't close."

"Was it as uncomfortable as the game at my place?"

Violet pinched her lips against a smile. "Maybe. Was it pretty bad over there?"

"Yes. Alison brought that scary vibe with her so I left in a hurry without thinking I might be running from the frying pan to the fire." Ryan glanced around. The other teams were focused on their own flavors, and he found he was glad the music helped with that. "Trevor didn't say a word the whole time, and Katie tried to cover with the most inane chatter. I mean, don't get me wrong. I generally like her. She seems good for Cameron. But apparently when she's tense she, like, narrates life."

"What do you mean?"

"Mostly she announced out loud every card that was played and what might beat it, also started describing the wood grain on the table at one point."

"Hmm. That does sound kind of painful." Violet seemed entertained.

Ryan thought it could be sort of entertaining in hindsight. But he hoped Violet was more entertained by his recounting.

"I'm just glad they made up quickly. It wouldn't be funny otherwise."

"Do you know what happened?" Ryan asked. He was a little curious because Trevor hadn't told him anything. He only knew things were patched up when Trevor was happier. Violet seemed interested though. He asked primarily to keep her talking.

Violet was almost ready to roll out the dough. "We want six from a batch, right?"

"Good memory," he said.

She smiled at the compliment and came around to the same side of the table to form the dough balls. That made it so they both had their backs to the others. Then she stood close enough to keep her voice low. "It sounds like Trevor made one too many critical remarks about her playing so she got mad and walked out in the middle of the game. But he showed up at her shop the next day to apologize in person, *got up early* to be there when she got there."

Ryan nodded at the significance in her voice. They all knew Trevor didn't get up early for anything. It was understandable that doing so would score points with Alison.

"She felt bad that she had handled it poorly anyway, and they agreed she should just tell him the next time he's being a jerk so he can fix it right away."

"Yeah. He knows he can be a little intense, especially when he's feeling competitive, so he'll back off if you say something."

"I'd still rather have you as a Tichu partner," Violet said. Then she quickly bent forward to better focus on the work in front of her.

Although he almost thought she was trying to hide her face. Was she embarrassed because she worried he might take "thanks for not yelling at me when we play cards" to mean something more like "let's start spending a lot more time together?" He used the break in the conversation to study his recipe and make sure he hadn't gotten too distracted by what Violet definitely did not say.

As soon as he was sure he hadn't left anything out, the pause made him realize what was playing in the background. "Wait a minute," he said. "This is a Christmas song."

Violet smiled at his surprise. "So? It's almost Christmas."

"It's almost *Thanksgiving*."

"They're not all Christmas songs," she said. "She only mixed in a few."

"Are you talking about the song?" Audra was suddenly on the other side of the table looking oddly excited about being caught playing Christmas music too early.

"He just noticed it was a Christmas song," Violet said.

"Did you tell him about Rosie?"

"Um... no."

"Okay, go ahead." Audra flashed a smile and returned to her pie table.

Ryan wasn't sure what the brief visit had been about. It seemed that Audra had been casually checking in, yet she had a strangely purposeful air about her.

"Rosie was kind of ridiculous about it," Violet started. She paused to give Ryan a chance to show whether or not he wanted to hear what Audra meant.

He didn't need to fake interest. Violet usually sounded torn between amusement and exasperation when she talked about her sister, and Ryan could easily relate to that mix of feelings.

"She keeps checking in with me to see what songs I picked for the reception," Violet said. "Her main reason seems to be to make sure I'm sticking to her stipulation of no Christmas songs. I admit I suggested a couple just to mess with her. So the one song she wanted to pick herself is the big, overorganized first dance thing, and she told me it was this one." Violet gestured over her shoulder to the source of the music.

"Was she kidding?"

"No, but I thought she was so I laughed. She hung up on me. I thought we were just disconnected somehow until I called her back and... Apparently, Nate suggested the song and Rosie liked it but was concerned people were going to accuse her of losing her identity because he talked her into a Christmas song after talking her into having music in the first place when no one else did. And no one else even really tried to convince her to do Christmas music, and it's just a song." Violet sighed at the drama.

52

Ryan had been listening but also trying to hear the song she was talking about. He could see it being appropriate for a December wedding. "I like it," he said. "Who sings it? Or was singing." It ended while he was asking.

"Phil Wickham. Oh, no!" Violet had torn the crust trying to get it to the pan. She managed to overlap enough to patch it.

Ryan stepped around her to roll out the next ball while she fluted the edges. "Nice save there."

"Thanks. I hope I'm not giving you the wrong idea when I complain about my sister and the wedding plans. She's normally much more... normal. I think she's getting nervous."

"Marriage is a big deal," he said. "It's understandable."

Audra returned. She looked between Violet and Ryan expectantly.

"What?" he asked.

"Just checking on the progress." Audra smiled, then fixed her eyes pointedly at Violet. Ryan couldn't tell if she got a reaction before she started talking again. "So all the talk about Christmas got me thinking about how we were going to do the decorations here on Friday and how maybe I'd rather spend my day off with Logan."

"I doubt it'll take more than an hour," Ryan said. "And he can help."

"He *could*... but I think he'd be about as excited about it as you are."

Ryan was not excited about it at all. That was why he'd enlisted Audra's help. She liked making things pretty. He expected that with her there he'd mostly stand around waiting to be asked to reach or lift things. But he might actually get done faster without all the careful consideration she'd put into the placements. "All right," he said. "I'll do it by myself."

"You *could*... but I have an even better idea." Her eyes shifted to Violet and back in a dead giveaway of what she was about to propose. "Violet is off this whole week. The studio is closed because so many families travel and miss class anyway and… She already said she was looking forward to getting our Christmas stuff out on Friday to have something to do. But we don't have that much for the apartment anyway. She would *love* to help you here." Audra nodded as though that was that before Ryan or Violet could respond.

He would have needed a minute to figure out what to say. It was one thing to argue with Audra about her trying to arrange time with Violet when it was just the two of them. It was another when Violet was standing right there. He couldn't honestly say he didn't want Violet's help and anything about how she didn't need to help just because Audra suggested it would sound like he didn't want her there. Audra had set him up to be more likely to offend Violet than accidentally reveal some interest.

"I, uh…" Violet had decided to venture into the silence. "I do like to decorate."

That changed the situation. A little. Audra hadn't just invented some excuse to throw them together if it was something Violet would actually like. "Okay," he said. "If you're saying you'd enjoy putting up most of the decorations for me, then I will accept your help."

She laughed, seemed to think it was funny that he wanted to get out of the work.

He asked what time she wanted to do his work for him, and she suggested right after lunch. He said he would drive. It was perfectly logical to ride together from the same building. Yet there was still a brief date-like vibe as it was arranged.

At least until Ryan noticed Grandma May standing in front of them grinning like a Cheshire cat. "How's the pumpkin coming?" he asked her.

"That boy's not as hopeless as he thinks," Grandma said, "but he does have quite a bit to learn."

Ryan nodded. "Good thing you're here."

"Well, I'm good, but I can't work a miracle with one lesson." Her eyes moved past him to Cameron for a moment, like she was watching a playful puppy. "We're working on stirring while keeping all the ingredients in the bowl."

He sensed Violet turning to check Cameron's progress. She smiled as though she also thought his incompetence was adorable, which got under Ryan's skin. It made him wonder if she'd noticed how well he'd stirred their filling. And that was annoying, too, because stirring wasn't a skill that should impress anyone. It wasn't even a skill.

"I need to get back. I just popped over here because Audra told me that you two are getting my decorations up on Friday. Is that right?" She glanced between them.

Violet only nodded.

"Of course, Grandma. I know the tradition." He knew she always put the restaurant decorations up the Friday after Thanksgiving. The ones at her house had much more flexibility.

"Good. Great. I look forward to seeing your take on Christmas at the January Café." She left the table with a giddy wave. The way she'd examined Violet suggested that she hadn't come to confirm the decorations at all, nor was it the decorations she thought were more exciting than stirring.

Now Ryan had to wonder how long it would take before Violet got fed up and told everyone to stop dreaming.

6

That one curl was doing something weird. Violet had just pinned up her hair, and most of the dark curls spilled nicely over her head. But one section near the back had ended up too short to spill and was floating side to side as she moved her head. Was she being too critical? It wasn't a date. And it wasn't as though Ryan was going to fall in love with her based on what that one section of her hair was doing today. He wasn't going to come to Rosie's wedding or not based on a weird curl. The situation had taken on enough urgency to make Violet slightly irrational. She was still convincing herself not to re-pin her hair as she walked away from the mirror.

Ryan had texted that he'd be ready in ten minutes. Two or three of those minutes had been used on her hair. She didn't have many left for shoes, coat and a few words with Audra. If she wasn't fast enough and Ryan showed up at the door for her, Violet's stomach butterflies were going to stop dancing and start exploding.

She bundled up and stepped into the living room. Plastic crinkled under her shoes. Audra was painting, which meant she was standing in the middle of a crinkle factory. The carpet, the furniture and even most of the walls were covered in plastic sheets. Audra was not a messy painter, but she knew paint could drip or splash. That was just a fact. Violet thought all the noise it made when she shifted around her work would be distracting. Audra had no trouble tuning it out. She dropped her brush into a can when she noticed Violet.

"You ready?" The light in her eyes was even brighter than her smile.

"We're just going to put up decorations."

"Aw. Ryan said exactly the same thing," Audra said. "That's why I know today will be awesome."

Violet shook her head at her roommate's optimism. Ryan would have said it to warn Audra not to get her hopes up. Violet said it to keep her own hopes down. The two statements were completely different. And Violet didn't have time to explain what Audra already knew. "Well, I hope you and Logan have fun."

"Oh, he'll be bored in five minutes. But at least he won't ask to watch me paint again."

"Are you planning to give him a boring day on purpose?"

"That's not up to me," Audra said. She pointed a finger up, meaning God was in charge of her inspiration.

Though she'd never sat down and actually watched her — because Audra didn't like anyone watching her paint — Violet had been around enough to know that sometimes she worked quickly and brilliantly. Pictures just appeared on the canvas in front of her. On other days, she spent a lot of time staring at paint and scraping off or covering up things that weren't working for her. Logan was not one for sitting still, but Audra had never let him watch before. Even a boring day would make him happy.

"I guess if Ryan's estimate is right, I'll be back in a little over an hour," Violet said as she turned to leave.

Audra responded with a highly skeptical raised eyebrow. She expected Violet and Ryan to be having so much fun that at least one of them made excuses to hang out together much longer.

Violet snorted at the expression, then waved. She didn't bother to lock the door behind her as it was difficult to do with gloves on. Audra could lock it easier from inside if she wanted, and Logan was expected soon anyway. The good thing about the cold was that Violet thought it was too cold to blush. She smiled confidently at

Ryan when he appeared around the corner a moment later. He was cute in his Ohio State hat with the red-and-white ball of fluff on top.

"You haven't been waiting for me, have you?" he asked, clearly concerned about her being out in the cold.

"No. Just stepped outside."

"Good. Let's go." He motioned her alongside him as he walked to his car. Tindee was a very small town so they only had a few minutes to chat about how the car wouldn't have time to warm up before they drove across it. Ryan mentioned there was a possibility they'd see an inch of snow later. Violet had heard it described as a dusting, which was basically the same.

Ryan parked behind the January Café, on January Street. Violet had never entered through the back. It was solid brick with a gray metal door. Ryan's keys jingled as he unlocked it. The door looked heavy, but he pulled it open easily and tipped his head to indicate Violet should go in ahead of him. He reached behind her as he entered to flip on a light before moving to unlock the office.

It had only been a few days since they were here making pies. The kitchen looked different clean and darker – Ryan hadn't turned on all the lights – and empty. Empty except for Ryan. His access to this closed business highlighted his responsibility. It gave him an air of dependability and trustworthiness and maybe a few other attributes that caused Violet to fight off some swooniness to hear what he was saying.

"Most of the decorations are in here."

Violet followed to the office doorway and peeked inside. The desk was neat but old, made of worn wood. A comfortable-looking chair pushed up to it stood out as the only thing that might be less than several decades old. A five-drawer filing cabinet had only its top drawer flush. The others were either crooked or slightly ajar. Ryan had walked over to a floor-to-ceiling cabinet in the back. The paint on the wooden doors was chipped and one of the handles wiggled when he tugged it open.

"I think my grandma had this built just to hold the Christmas decorations," Ryan said. "There isn't much else in it. I wonder if she knows about those shoes. They must be hers." He pointed to a pair of women's sandals wedged next to a box on the bottom shelf.

Some of the boxes had words written in black marker. Ryan pulled out one that said TREE. "This actually means ornaments for the tree. The tree itself is probably the only thing not in here. It's, uh, well, going to take me a few minutes to get it down. Why don't you go ahead and take a look in some of these boxes, see if you have any ideas on where to put anything. Then we'll get started when I have the tree."

"Okay," Violet said. She waited for him to exit before she went into the office and approached the boxes. She grabbed one labeled GARLAND and pulled it out enough to lift the lid. There were several spools of red and silver tinsel garland and some plastic holly. That box had a lot of possibilities. The next one was labeled TABLES. Violet found menu holders shaped like Christmas trees and sparkly red salt shakers next to sparkly green pepper shakers. She set that box by the door as an obvious place to start. No one would need to think too hard about where to put those items.

An occasional banging or scraping noise came from the other side of the kitchen. Violet was curious about where exactly the Christmas tree was stashed and what Ryan had to do to get it. But he'd asked her to check out the boxes, and she was equally curious about the rest of the contents. She got down the box of tree ornaments with barely a peek inside because they would need whatever was in there. A box that did require investigation had only the word CHRISTMAS printed on its side. She found some clingy things for the windows, a mini tree, plastic candy canes in various sizes and other miscellaneous décor. There was a book of some sort at the very bottom. Violet dug it out and turned it over on her lap.

It was a photo album. A picture of the Norman family was inserted into a pocket on the cover. The baby in the pink dress must be Audra with Trevor and Ryan as little boys. Violet wouldn't have recognized any of them if she didn't know what their parents looked like, or at least what they looked like twenty or so years after the picture was taken.

"What's that?"

Violet jumped at the sound of Ryan's voice from the doorway. She flushed with guilt at being caught with a personal album, even though she'd just figured out what it was and hadn't even considered whether or not to open it.

Ryan came closer to see.

"It was in the box of Christmas stuff," Violet explained. "I… um…"

Ryan laughed when he saw the picture. He didn't seem at all upset that she had it. "Oh, that's right. I remember my grandma saying at some point that she kept some pictures here. She thought if, God forbid, anything ever happened to their house, they wouldn't lose all the pictures."

Violet thought that was smart. A little morbid, but smart. "That makes sense," she said.

"Yeah." Ryan nodded. "Except maybe the part about keeping it with the Christmas stuff."

Violet laughed and since she'd relaxed, she tapped the picture and said, "You look a little like your dad here."

"I guess. Does he look like a guy who's smart enough to realize *before* he puts the ladder away that he'll need it again to put the box back?"

The meaning of the question made Violet smile again as she put the album in the box and got to her feet. But there was something else that made her smile. Ryan seemed to be in a very good mood for someone who did not enjoy putting up decorations. Was there any chance he was actually trying to be funny to impress her? It was unlikely – at least outside of a general guys like to impress

60

people sense – but it was a nice thought anyway. "So you want to do the tree first?" she asked.

He glanced at the big box he'd left outside the door. "Can you get the ornament box while I get this one?"

"Sure."

"It's not too heavy for you?"

"No." Violet picked up the box and waited until he turned away to roll her eyes. Of course it wasn't too heavy. It probably wasn't more than five pounds. To be fair though, it was possible he asked because he hadn't lifted it yet.

Ryan balanced the tree box on his shoulder and led the way into the dining room. Violet followed wondering how much that box weighed and whether or not Ryan could carry her with one arm like that. She immediately banished scenarios where he might try from her head to focus on the serious business at hand. Not that decorations were all that serious, but she had volunteered to do a job, and she was going to do it without any silly daydreaming.

Ryan opened his box as soon as he set it down. "The tree is one thing I know how to do so we should have this up in a minute. Unless you think we should put it somewhere else?" It was clear he wasn't just trying to be polite and sincerely wanted her opinion.

Violet surveyed the room and shared her thoughts as they came to her. "I think that back corner is the only other place we could put it without moving tables. But up here, people can see it better through the window, and there's an outlet right there for the lights."

"Those are probably the reasons Grandma usually puts it here."

"If it ain't broke," Violet said.

Ryan nodded and grabbed the base for the tree from the box. Violet handed him parts, and they had a six-foot tree assembled in very little time. The lights were on top of the ornament box.

"I hope these work," Violet said as she picked up the string.

Something small and plastic hit the ground. And then another one like it. She held the lights steady while she tried to figure out what she was dropping. "Oh, they have… covers." They weren't covers exactly but a clear plastic star slipped around each bulb.

Ryan picked them up for her while she tried to find the lights missing stars.

Another hit the floor as she turned the string. "Oops." She sent him an apologetic look.

He held the pieces gingerly and appeared far less sure of himself than he'd been while setting up the tree. "Maybe you put them on the tree and point out the ones missing covers to me as you go?"

Violet shrugged. "Okay." She was happy to find that they did light up. There were only a few on the tree when she found the first one needing a cover. Ryan fit one on, and she noticed how close he was to her. There wasn't much room to work tethered by a string of lights. He smelled nice, mildly spicy. He stayed right at her elbow as she pointed out another missing star. She was having trouble thinking about anything except how close he was. Until the clink of plastic hitting the floor was enough of a distraction. She seemed to be dropping one star for every one Ryan replaced. Her leg brushed a lower branch and knocked off one they might have already replaced.

Violet was afraid Ryan was getting frustrated, and that was the only thing that kept her from laughing. Then he dropped one as he was trying to put it on. When he reached under the tree for it, his sleeve caught another and sent it skittering several feet across the floor. That's when he lost his composure, which gave Violet permission to laugh, too.

"What is wrong with these things?" Violet asked, still trying to catch her breath. "Were they this much trouble last year?"

"I don't know. I just put up the tree, then Grandma and Audra decorated it."

"They don't seem to fit very well."

"No, they don't." He examined the pieces in his hand with a thoughtful expression. "I think I've seen these on the tree for quite a few years. I wonder if Grandma pulled them off lights that burned out at some point and put them on a new string. If they didn't come together, it might explain why they don't want to stay together."

"Yeah." Violet guessed it was a 200-light string, and she was still holding half of it, waiting for Ryan to suggest they keep working.

He held up a plastic star. "Do you like these? I mean, do you think they're pretty?"

She hadn't seen anything like them so she liked that they were unique. But they weren't especially attractive. She shrugged, and that somehow made one fall off the other side of the tree.

"I think I'm going to use my authority to decree that we take off all the stupid little plastic things and just hang plain lights this year."

Violet nodded. She saw no reason to argue with that. "What do you want to do with the stars?"

"I don't think I should say what I *want* to do with them. But I'll run into the kitchen for a bag. We'll leave them in the box for now."

Violet continued to stare where Ryan was as he left, fixing the playfully threatening expression in her memory for later enjoyment.

"You don't have to wait for me." He'd stopped partway to the kitchen. "Just keep hanging the lights, and I'll start collecting stars when I get back."

"Okay." Violet quickly resumed her work, relieved that her immobility had been interpreted as patience instead of mooning. The only problem with not picking up the fallen plastic as she went was not stepping on them. She had to pay attention to the lights and the branches and the floor. All that kept her mind off Ryan as he gathered up all those stars. She finished first and pulled off a handful of the ones at the end of the string. He held open the bag to her.

Violet dropped the pieces in. She felt some serious electricity at having their hands nearly touching. It seemed a good idea to let him collect the rest while she checked out the ornaments.

They were mostly classic bulbs of red and green and silver. A few bows and some tinsel made the tree even prettier. Ryan stood back to watch until Violet got to the last item in the box, a shoebox she assumed didn't have shoes.

"That should be the manger," he said.

She must have looked puzzled because he explained.

"Grandma likes to put a manger under the tree to remind people of the real gift. Does it at home, too."

Violet remembered seeing that last year now that he mentioned it. She found pieces of wood on top of paper straw when she took the lid off the small box. She sat down to work on assembling the manger. Two shorter pieces were the ends. The long skinny pieces must be used to make the sides. There were slots the side pieces fit into, but she wasn't seeing what would make it all stable. The ends would tip over and cause the sides to fall out. She looked up at Ryan. "Do you know how this works?"

"No." He lowered himself to sit next to her. "If I had known last year that I'd be in charge this year, I'd have paid more attention."

The pieces Violet set up fell apart as she expected. She didn't try again right away. "They really never talked to you about taking over before they offered it to you?"

He shook his head. "When they decided to hire a manager to cut their hours back, I was still in high school. Once Matt was doing a good job, there was no reason to consider anyone else until he decided to move."

"Were you... nervous that you might screw it up?"

"Thanks."

"I didn't say I thought you would. It's just... The January Café is kind of a big deal in town. I'd think there'd be some pressure."

"I knew what you meant." His eyes danced to confirm he'd

been teasing before he got more serious. "I'm sure I'd have felt pressure if my grandparents were handing over the reins and then disappearing. But they're still pretty involved so I knew they'd have my back."

"True."

"In fact, that was…" Ryan took a breath, seemed to be choosing his words. "I'll tell you the one thing that worried me was that with them here to open and me not needed until mid-morning, I thought I'd be tempted to sleep in. Then I'd be here until at least seven and I'd come home too tired to really feel like doing anything else and this place would become my whole life. But I've actually been getting up earlier. I joined a 6 AM men's group at church on Thursdays, and I get in a run most other days. Then I have time to read or practice some songs or something, and I sometimes come in early to hang out with my grandpa and his friends. They're kind of hilarious."

Violet smiled. "Audra has told me some stories."

"Yeah, so… even though I don't do much in the evenings, I've already squeezed in some life before work."

"You do seem happier since starting here," Violet observed. She quickly dropped her eyes to the manger parts she was fingering. That was a mushy thing to say, and it might reveal that she'd been paying a lot of attention.

He didn't say anything as he picked up some of the other parts. He held one end and one side while she tried to fit the other side and end into place.

Violet glanced up. Ryan appeared to be concentrating on the puzzle in front of them. His mind was probably not replaying the last bits of the conversation. While it was good that he didn't seem freaked out by her comment, and while she was glad that he was happy, it occurred to her that it could mean he wasn't looking for anything – anyone – to add to his life.

The project eventually took over Violet's attention as well.

With four parts together, Ryan held it with one hand and added another strip to one side. Violet carefully copied on the other side. It stayed together when they each had a hand on one end. A few glances communicated it was time to let go. Both ends tipped over and the sides clattered to the floor. They started laughing together.

"Are you sure this is all the parts?" Ryan asked.

"Yeah, I... oh." Violet had pulled the box closer to point out that there was only paper straw left, and she caught sight of something slide across the bottom. There was another piece of wood under the straw. "Oops," she said as she got it out.

Ryan thought it was funny, but at the current rate, he wasn't going to be saying he owed her one anytime soon.

The bottom piece had grooves that the others fit into and held it all in place. Violet stuffed in the straw and pushed it under the tree. She got to her feet to put the embarrassment behind her. "What's next?" she said.

"You tell me." He led the way back to the office to sort through the other boxes. The salt and pepper shakers had apparently not been used for a few years. Ryan assigned himself the job of washing and filling them. He stayed in the kitchen while Violet draped garland along the counter. She found some silver snowflakes to hang from the ceiling and a few odds and ends of Christmas charm. She noticed Ryan gathering up the boring salt and pepper shakers at some point. The place was looking very festive as she got a wreath of holly straightened on the wall. She stepped back to survey her work and noticed the red and green shakers on the tables. How had she missed Ryan putting them out? Oh. And how long had he been watching her?

She walked towards the back counter feeling self-conscious. There was something off about his expression, something she couldn't read. He pushed himself away from the counter when she was close. "It looks great in here," he said. "Are we done?"

"Yeah." She was done, but she would have said so regardless

because he somehow gave the impression that the question was rhetorical, that he was done.

Violet followed him back to the kitchen. Ryan went into the office long enough to put back the last box and close the cabinet. He turned off the lights and locked up behind her. Violet got into the car wondering why there was suddenly weird tension between them. Maybe it was the time. They'd been there about two hours, and Violet hadn't realized it had been that long. Maybe he'd been watching her repositioning that plastic holly thinking that no one would care if it was off-center.

She fiddled with her zipper, actually tempted to laugh because she could so clearly picture Audra yelling at her for wasting these two hours. Plenty of opportunities to mention the wedding had been squandered. Violet had kept thinking about it and kept telling herself it would be better to wait. She hadn't asked Ryan which treat he'd prefer for his birthday either, hadn't even thought about asking that because she'd been so preoccupied with *not* asking if he'd go to Rosie's wedding.

As the car slowed, Violet worried they were about to have an awkward parting. If she was too quiet or unnatural, it would appear she was mad at him for being mad at nobody knew what. Awkward.

"Violet," he said as he turned off the car. "I want to make sure I say thank you for your help today. I really didn't want to do all that myself so... I do appreciate it."

He sounded sincere. Maybe he hadn't been upset about the time at all. Regardless, the gratitude was an opening. She could teasingly ask if he wanted a chance to return the favor. Explain how Rosie put her in a bind. "You're welcome," she said. "I do like all the pretty Christmas stuff. Except for those stars on the lights."

Ryan smiled at the reminder. "Yeah. I suggest we don't mention how much trouble we had with those because I can't imagine they'd still be around if everyone else has always struggled so much."

It hadn't occurred to Violet to wonder how anyone got those stars in the box without them falling off. Ryan had a good point. Though she didn't understand what they could have done wrong, it made her smile to think they did it wrong together.

He opened his door so Violet did the same. She moved slowly enough that he could come around and start up the brick walk with her.

"I guess we can expect you and the other ladies to check in on our Tichu game at some point tonight?"

That was a great time to ask about a birthday treat. His birthday was actually Saturday, but she and Audra planned to bring something to acknowledge it while everyone was together. "Audra will insist," she said. She almost had the courage to say Audra would insist on something else when Audra herself popped out of the house still getting her arms in her coat.

"Hi, guys!" Audra bounded off the porch and landed on the sidewalk that went around to Ryan's side, presumably to cut him off. "I'm glad you're back because I've been kicking myself so hard about what I realized this afternoon. I've been trying to tell both of you that it's a great idea for Ryan to go to Rosie's wedding. Violet will be embarrassed to go by herself, not because she should be but because Rosie's turning it into a big deal with a dance that highlights… And anyway, Ryan likes to dance and even knows how to waltz, learned it for a musical he did in high school. He'd have fun while making himself useful, which I know he also likes. So I haven't been able to understand why you guys weren't seeing my brilliance and then boom! It hit me this afternoon that Ryan works on Saturdays. I don't know why neither of you told me that was the problem, but I already know an easy solution. I will cover for you. It's no problem for me to come in and be the pretend boss for a few hours next Saturday. Don't worry about me making a big sacrifice by leaving my paintings early. It's no problem. Really. Now it's all worked out.

"I'll go back inside so you can talk about how I was an idiot for not realizing the problem sooner. But mostly talk about how it's perfect now." She gave them each one firm look to reinforce that they were being left with instructions, then dashed back into the house.

"Do you, uh... First of all, did you follow all that?" Ryan seemed slightly dazed, as though Audra had just come out and spun him around a few times.

Violet nodded slowly. She was still catching up, too. But she noticed that the primary effect of Audra's speech was that it left her unable to focus on how nervous she was. Violet followed her example of talking fast. "It really would be so nice of you if you could go to the wedding. I wouldn't have minded being by myself except that yesterday Rosie decided it would be awkward to have Mom sit out after all so she plans to find someone else last minute for me, and I just know who it'll be because as far as I know, Nate only has one single friend who's coming and I've only met him once but he just got on my nerves and it would be so much better if you would please say you'll go. Unless it's too much to ask, then you don't have to."

Ryan opened his mouth but didn't immediately say anything. A word was trying to come out.

Violet waited in suspense.

Finally, he said, "Okay."

"Okay?"

"Yeah. That's not too much to ask, especially if Audra's volunteering to cover for me at work."

"Great. Thank you. Um, I'm going inside where it's warm now."

He nodded and moved towards his door with a wave.

Violet rushed inside, a little embarrassed over the abrupt ending but elated at the success. She'd finally asked, and he hadn't refused. She was going to worry about how scary that was later.

7

Ryan checked the time before he began to fan out his cards. It was only three minutes after the last time he checked, which was probably why Logan was smirking at him.

"Waiting for someone?" he asked.

The question sounded rhetorical, and Ryan judged it best to treat it that way regardless. There was no point getting everyone talking about Violet before she even got there. He was already concerned about what Audra would say.

"Audra's pretty proud of her matchmaking," Logan said.

"Yeah, I heard you're taking Violet to her sister's wedding tomorrow," Trevor added.

Ryan looked across the table at Cameron, who did not appear surprised. Then he asked Trevor when he heard that.

"Alison said something about it the other day."

"And you wait until Violet's about to come over to bring it up?"

Trevor pointed at Logan. "*He* brought it up."

"The wedding is not a result of anyone's matchmaking," Ryan said.

Trevor looked confused.

Logan said, "You mean you taking Violet?"

"Yes. I'm not… Violet's sister told her that if she showed up alone that she'd pair her up with some guy Violet doesn't like. That's the only reason I'm going. Because I'm less irritating than this other guy." Ryan put down the cards he wanted to pass.

Cameron and Trevor already had theirs on the table.

Logan set down one card. He seemed to be struggling over the other choices. Then he turned back to Ryan and asked, "Are you sure?"

"Am I sure about what?"

"About the reason… Audra thinks…"

There was no reason for Logan to finish that sentence. "I know what Audra thinks," Ryan said. "She's been impossible all week. She's told everyone – even the employees who won't be there – how she's going to be in charge instead of me on Saturday and her impression of why. She's making it sound so… I swear she couldn't be making a bigger deal if I was the one actually getting married."

"It could be something," Trevor said, wiggling a card on the table to tell Logan to hurry up. "I mean, a wedding might be a good setting to spark something."

The other guys had the nerve to nod as though they had any idea what they were talking about.

"Only if there was something to spark," Ryan said. He played a straight to start. "She asked me to protect her from Mr. Irritating. I'm pretty sure that's a job for someone she's sure won't get the wrong idea."

Even Trevor looked as though that was a good point. Unfortunately.

"I don't know, man. I wouldn't give up completely," Logan said. "You're going to get all dressed up for her. Girls like that. She might get swoony."

They were keeping the game going while they talked, but Ryan paused to raise an eyebrow at Logan before he beat the pair on the table. "Did you just use the word swoony?"

"He did." Trevor sounded disapproving.

"Doesn't to swoon mean to faint?" Cameron asked. "Is that a good thing?"

"Depends on the girl," Logan said.

"And whether or not she actually faints." Trevor collected a trick with his words.

Ryan was shaking his head at the unbelievable turn of this conversation. And it was only getting started.

"I think swoony is one of those words that's changed meaning over time. Women would literally faint when they got excited about something back when they were all wearing corsets and couldn't breathe properly. According to Alyssa, they would sometimes pretend to faint so a guy would have to catch them." Logan sounded surprisingly scholarly giving this definition he'd apparently heard from his middle-school-aged sister. "Now it can mean to faint or just be attracted to someone."

"So whether or not it's a good thing depends on if Ryan wants her to be swoony," Cameron observed.

"Stop saying swoony." Ryan was uncomfortable because he was distracted by thoughts of catching Violet.

Trevor tossed his remaining cards on the table. "Sounds like a yes to me."

"I got forty-five."

"Fifteen here," Cameron said.

"Sixty for you, forty for us?" Logan confirmed. He got nods all around.

"The only thing that matters," Ryan said, "is that Violet is going to find you even more irritating than the other guy if you're talking like I might be getting the wrong idea in front of her."

"Definitely a yes," Trevor said. He reached out a hand for the cards Logan was shuffling.

Logan passed the cards. "But what if... you were getting the right idea?"

"I don't have any ideas," Ryan said. It was probably the truest thing anyone had said all night, yet it was still annoying that the other guys looked as though it was the truest thing anyone had said all night. "Just lay off when the girls are here."

Logan opened his mouth but thought better of whatever he was going to say. The guys sorted their cards in silence. Ryan resisted the urge to check the time again. The doorbell signaled the arrival they expected when the round had barely begun. Audra came in practically singing hello. Alison was right behind her with her mom, who sometimes came along to watch the game.

"Good evening, gentlemen," she said.

The guys nodded or waved.

Katie and Violet came in last. Their arms were linked in a way that suggested Violet was somewhat reluctant to enter. She smiled at Ryan, then bit the side of her lip as her eyes moved around the room. He assumed that she'd already endured some teasing along the same lines as he had. It might be a good idea to let her know that he wasn't confused about their relationship just because their friends were. But he was worried about beginning a conversation like that. What if he accidentally implied there was something wrong with her that made him not wish for a romantic shift? And it'd be hard to say anything without lying. Better to hope everyone would leave her alone when it became clear that the wedding didn't "spark something."

"You guys are unusually quiet," Audra said. Her eyes scanned the room suspiciously.

Trevor narrowed his eyes at her. "We don't need a lot of chatter to keep a game going."

"Yeah, I know, but... I sense you all got quiet right as we came in." She put a hand on Logan's arm.

"I sense you are imagining things," he said.

A few people chuckled. Ryan hoped that would be the end of the scrutiny. Yes, they had been talking about Violet. But there had been a natural end to the conversation. There was no guilty silence. Except that he felt a little guilty once Audra brought it up. Someone needed to say something unrelated.

Alison's mom addressed Trevor. "You coming to the house before your next appointment for discerning the vocation of marriage with my daughter?"

Trevor's eyes got a little wider, but he didn't say anything.

"She means date," Alison said.

Trevor nodded, then shook his head.

"I like your mom's way of saying it," Audra said, "but it is a mouthful."

"He means he's not, Mom. And now I'm taking this mouthful home with me. Goodnight, everyone." Alison waved and gently shoved her mom towards the door. There was a general chorus of goodbyes as they left.

Ryan thought Trevor had an interesting relationship with his possible future mother-in-law, which was also kind of a mouthful. He'd told Alison she was creepy before he knew who she was. Now she seemed to enjoy occasionally saying slightly outrageous things to him to watch for a response.

As soon as the door closed, Trevor said, "I think we're still playing a game." He was probably trying to deflect any comments about the interesting relationship.

They were playing a game though. Ryan realized he was the only one who had won any tricks so it must be his lead. He didn't think he was going to win any more, and he was right. He hoped Violet noticed that he hadn't wasted his few good cards. He had earned some points for his team.

"Ryan." Audra said his name with the tone of someone getting attention for a very important question.

He was prepared for something frivolous. "Yes?"

"You are going to wear a suit tomorrow, right?"

Logan kept shuffling as he smiled at the question that wasn't funny.

"I guessed that would be expected," Ryan said.

"Because I don't remember the last time I saw you wear a tie," Audra said. "Do you even have a suit?"

"Yes." He had exactly one suit. It was purchased for job interviews near the end of college, and he only recently fit into it again. She only needed to know he had one, and he wasn't entirely sure she needed to know that much. Audra wasn't going to be there.

"Is it black?" she asked.

"Does it matter?"

Audra raised her hand to her hip. She looked over his shoulder to Violet for a moment. Then she said, "Do I need to pick a tie for you or do you only have one of those, too?"

Rather than answer her, he turned to Violet. "Do *you* have any concerns about my ability to dress myself?"

She laughed and said, "No."

That settled it. Ryan motioned Logan to give the cards to Cameron so they could get another round started.

Audra used the time it took him to deal to continue her interrogation. "You're not going to embarrass Violet, are you?"

"What?"

She shrugged like it was an innocent and perfectly reasonable question.

Katie tried not to laugh. Trevor did laugh.

"Seriously, what do you think I might do to embarrass her?"

"Well... I just... It would be bad if anyone knew you were a, um, a last-minute guest."

"Why?" Ryan asked. "And how would that even come up? You think someone is going to ask me exactly when I agreed to go?"

"No, but..."

He turned to Violet. "Isn't your sister the one who just told you last week that you needed to bring someone?"

"Yeah. It's not a big deal and... I think Audra is worried about something she doesn't need to worry about." Violet lifted her eyes to aim a warning at Audra the moment she started talking about her.

"I think… a little worry is a good idea."

"No. Not even a little."

"It would help."

The conversation had gotten weird. Ryan got the impression that Violet and Audra were going back and forth about something other than what they were actually saying. He had a handful of cards by now so he tuned out the words to focus on the game. The game made sense. Maybe they'd let him know if they decided something and if it had anything to do with him.

The round was somewhat exciting – Cameron bombed Logan's bomb – and that got the visitors talking about things Ryan understood. The round after that scored him and Cameron enough points to win. It was late enough to call it a night. Violet evidently agreed. She seemed to want to be the first one out to avoid being a fifth wheel when Audra and Katie wanted to walk out with Logan and Cameron.

She tapped Ryan's shoulder and leaned in long enough to whisper, "See you tomorrow," before she pretty much ran out the door.

He didn't have time to say anything in response. He only sat there thinking about the next day. He was going to a wedding with Violet. He would sit next to her in the church, dance with her at the reception, listen to her speech. When it was all over, he would have to tell her he enjoyed it without admitting how much he enjoyed it. That really wasn't the fun kind of challenge.

****

There weren't many cars in the lot when Ryan parked by the church. He was early, but he understood it wasn't going to be a very large wedding. The morning was bright, yet snow flurries were coming from somewhere. Ryan stuffed his hands in his pockets to keep them warm as he rushed to the door. He had barely made it inside when a woman's voice called his name.

It wasn't Violet. She was supposed to be helping her sister get ready. He hadn't expected to see her right away but realized with the disappointment that he'd still hoped for it.

"Hi, Sofia. Ben." Ryan nodded at the guy with the woman who had called his name. "I haven't seen either of you in a while."

"Yeah, I don't know," Sofia said. "We might officially be choir dropouts now."

That was how Ryan knew the couple. They both sang in the church choir with him. "How are you? I don't think I've seen you since the wedding so I should say congratulations."

"Thanks," Ben said.

Sofia grabbed Ben's hand and squeezed it excitedly. "Three months!" she said. "Obviously, we're doing well. How about you?"

"Not too much to complain about."

They were standing in a gathering space. Sofia gestured towards the sanctuary entrance. "Are you a friend of the bride or the groom?"

"Uh… the bride's sister actually."

"Oh." She smiled in a way that said she assumed he meant more than a friend. "That's nice. Her name's Violet, right?"

"Yes." Ryan was only confirming the name.

"We're here for the groom. Ben and Nate have been friends for years."

An older couple came through the outer door with a blast of cold air. Ryan let that push him forward to get out of their way. "Well, I hope you guys enjoy the wedding. Maybe we'll catch up more after."

"Yeah, that'd be great."

Ben nodded. They both stayed by the door. Ryan wondered briefly who they were waiting for before putting them out of his head.

A boy who looked about twelve and less comfortable in a suit than Ryan handed him a program as he stepped through the door. There were not many people in the church though they were clustered more towards the front than on a typical Sunday. Violet had told Ryan to sit in the second pew on the left. She would join him there after the procession. There was no one else in the reserved section, and he felt awkward claiming a seat there. He followed Violet's directions anyway.

The volume in the church increased gradually as more guests arrived and various chats broke out. It wasn't long before someone began to play a cello from the choir loft. People kept talking, but Ryan could no longer hear what they were saying over the music. He remained tense as the start time got close.

An organ was playing when a woman he guessed was Violet and Rosie's mom was escorted to the seat in front of him. She was shorter than Violet and her hair was straight and gray rather than curly and deep brown. But her eyes were so similar there was no way she wasn't related to Violet. The eye color was the same exact chocolate brown, too. Ryan got a good look because as soon as she was seated, she turned around and gave him a thorough once-over, then a nod of approval, before she faced front again.

The action was incredibly unnerving. But he reasoned that it was better than a look of disapproval. Probably. He didn't know what she approved of. It compounded the tension so he wasn't really paying attention to anything until Violet appeared in the aisle holding flowers.

She was beautiful. Her hair was braided from one side of her head around the back and over the other shoulder. Ryan couldn't remember seeing it not pinned up so he didn't know it was so long. She wore a black dress that had some red ribbons or threads woven in the sleeves. He knew Violet and Rosie had taken a long time to agree on a dress, and now he knew it had been worth the effort.

Rosie looked beautiful, too. It would have been hard not to while radiating so much happiness. Ryan still thought Violet upstaged her, but that was an opinion he would keep to himself for a variety of reasons. Before he knew it, Violet was sitting next to him. She'd tucked a program into the hymnal to follow along with the first reading. She got up to do the second one. Then she got up again to stand with her sister during the vows. The whole wedding Mass seemed to go by in a blink.

When Violet walked out with the recession, Ryan was feeling that his presence had been pointless. The first few people in the receiving line were monopolizing the wedding party. That made it simple for Ryan to slip around with other guests heading for the reception in the fellowship hall.

Round tables were set up with place cards. Ryan found his name next to Violet's. That should cover any actual concern about him looking like a last-minute guest. Violet's dad was on his other side. He hoped no one needed to be concerned about that either. Ryan wasn't going to sit there by himself so he wandered around until he ran into Sofia and Ben again. They were happy to share details about how their wedding compared to this one.

8

Violet thought the pictures must be taking longer than the entire ceremony. Her face hurt from smiling, and she was tired of being moved around like a chess piece. She knew, however, that everything was moving along right on schedule. She was only impatient to catch up to Ryan. He was here doing her a big favor, and she'd barely had a chance to say hello to him. Wait. Had she even said hello?

She'd been so focused on her duties she was afraid she hadn't said anything at all. The realization made her more impatient. Eventually, the photographer released everyone. According to Rosie's plan, she and Nate waited just outside the doors while the rest of the families went in and stood by the inside of the doors. People began to quiet as they noticed the bride and groom must be on their way. Violet's dad continued up to the microphone to make the announcement.

Violet's eyes searched the room for Ryan and found him chatting with a couple she'd just met. When they turned towards the incoming party, he took the opportunity to move closer to Violet. He seemed relieved to see her and was watching her when he paused to applaud the bride and groom with the rest of the guests.

After the official entrance, Ryan resumed his movement and Violet met him halfway. "Hi," she said.

"Are you exhausted yet?" he asked. "I think you've already had a very busy day."

"Well, I was up earlier than usual — too excited to sleep — so I'm probably going to crash eventually. But I think I'm still running on adrenaline right now." A big smile ignored her tired cheeks.

"You look, um... you look amazing."

"Thank you." Violet knew she blushed at the compliment. Even though it should not have been any different than when her dad told her she looked beautiful or her new brother-in-law told her she looked beautiful. It only meant he noticed that she was dressed up for a special occasion. Ryan was dressed up, too. The blue stripes in his tie matched his eyes and drew attention to his very nice eyes, and there was no way she was going to say she noticed that. "Let's, um..." She waved an arm towards their assigned table. "The plan is to serve lunch right away. Rosie and Nate are about to welcome everyone, then give us instructions for the buffet line."

They moved from the open area in the center of the large room towards a raised dais at one end. The microphone was set up on one side with a table only big enough for the newlyweds on the other. Violet and Ryan were assigned to a round table right in front of it with her parents, who were not around. They must be mingling. The table was large enough for eight, but the other half was empty. The bride's family could be on display there and guests could easily stop by to chat without interrupting conversations at the table. Violet held her tongue regarding her thoughts on this arrangement.

Ryan followed her to the seats. Violet tried to feel confident because she knew more of what to expect at the event and not nervous for not knowing what to expect from him. Audra was still hopeful. Violet knew she'd stop meddling if Ryan made it clear there was no chance whatsoever. But she couldn't be sure Audra wasn't just refusing to hear that.

Someone had switched the place cards. Violet had put herself between Ryan and her parents, and now they were reversed. She resisted the urge to lunge forward and change them back. That would invite questions about why she thought someone would think the switch was funny. She simply took her assigned seat. Maybe her parents would spend most of the time visiting at other tables anyway. Not that there was anything wrong with Violet's parents. She was afraid she might have said something around them that would make them think she was interested in Ryan as more than Audra's brother who was willing to fill in the dance. And they could hint at that from anywhere at the table.

Nate and Rosie had reached their table. Nate got a head start to the mic while Rosie arranged her bouquet as a centerpiece. He waited until she was by his side to welcome the guests. He explained that the caterers – the people in black aprons – were going to invite people to the buffet lines one table at a time beginning with him and his new wife. He assured them he'd get things moving and jumped off the front of the dais, which couldn't have been more than a foot from the ground, and got a laugh for his eagerness. Rosie walked to the steps at the side and joined him more gracefully.

One of those aproned peopled approached Ryan to say he and Violet could line up behind the bride. He stood and extended a hand to Violet before motioning to the left. He was only encouraging her to go first, but for a second it looked as though he was offering a hand to help her stand. Her stomach flipped at the thought. She was already trying not to think about dancing with him. She realized as she stood that she was still clutching her bouquet.

"Oh, um… I guess I should leave this here."

Ryan waited while she set the flowers somewhat clumsily at the edge of the table, then he walked quietly beside her. The whole room seemed quiet, as though everyone was watching Violet to see how she would mess up the date that wasn't a date. Of course she knew that wasn't true. If anyone had the guests' attention, it was the woman in the pretty white dress.

Violet didn't see her parents until they showed up at the food line at the same time. She smiled to acknowledge them.

Her mom smiled back.

Her dad said, "Food," as he picked up a plate right behind Rosie.

Violet gestured for her mom to go after him and Ryan made a similar gesture at Violet. The food looked good but somehow merely decorative to Violet. She had no appetite. It wasn't just Ryan. It was the speech she had to give, and the notecards she'd left at home because she'd practiced so much she knew she had everything memorized, and the sudden certainty that she would forget every word the moment she stood in front of everyone. She skipped the sandwiches and took a spoonful of fruit salad and a few crackers. Hopefully, that would be enough to keep her strength up without risking the food itself coming up.

Violet's mom leaned towards her, bumped her eyebrows up and down and said, "So that's him."

Violet sucked in a breath and glanced at Ryan. He appeared to have not heard. Her mom's tone had not said, "That's the guy you talked into coming at the last minute." It said, "That's the guy you've been gushing about." Violet had probably mentioned him, just like she'd mentioned Trevor and Logan and Cameron, because they were guys she saw somewhat regularly. She hadn't gushed.

"Yes, that's Ryan," she whispered back. "Audra's brother."

Her mom nodded and turned away with her plate.

Violet paused to let Ryan catch up.

"Not very hungry?" he said.

"I'm too nervous to eat."

His expression was full of sympathy. "Maybe you can get seconds after your speech."

She nodded and said, "Cake."

That made him laugh. They were still setting their plates on the table when Violet's dad looked between them with a rather stern expression. "I believe introductions are in order."

Violet pulled out her chair as she complied. "This is Audra's brother, Ryan Norman. Ryan, these are my parents, George and Jen Neuman."

"It's nice to meet you both," Ryan said as he took his seat.

Violet's mom smiled at him. "Same here."

Her dad set down his fork. "You are the manager at the January Café?" he asked.

"Yes."

"I understand that's a family business."

"Yes. My grandparents own it."

"Do they intend to pass full ownership to you?"

Ryan glanced at Violet as he slipped his napkin onto his lap. "I... That has recently become their intent, although I don't expect it to happen immediately."

"Small businesses can be tricky to keep afloat," he said. "Do you think it can support a family?"

"Uh, Dad?" Violet interrupted. "I think you're getting a bit... personal here." She wanted to say he was getting way, way off track. Ryan had not expressed the slightest bit of interest in his daughter so the man had no right to grill him as though he was about to propose. But the line of questioning was embarrassing enough without explicitly stating how it sounded.

Her dad looked at Ryan as though he hadn't heard and still expected an answer.

"We seem to have a pretty loyal customer base," Ryan said.

George Neuman grunted and half smiled. He seemed impressed despite himself at the cagey answer. "I know you are a member of this church," he said. "You sing in the choir." It was a clear statement, yet he eyed Ryan as though an answer was not optional.

"I joined when I was in college," Ryan spoke slowly, thinking about what to say, "though I couldn't attend regularly until I

84

graduated. I generally enjoy it."

"Generally?" Violet's dad pounced on this word with a raised eyebrow.

"I do enjoy it," Ryan said. "But I sometimes think the music director could pick up the pace."

"Oh, I know what you mean." Violet's mom jumped into the conversation. "Just this past Sunday, we were singing a song… What was it? There was a line about 'every peak and valley humming.'"

"*People, Look East,*" Ryan said.

"Right. That's the one. I was thinking to myself, 'Why does this song of joyful anticipation sound so sad?'"

Ryan nodded at her and Violet agreed, too. Her dad frowned as though they were not helping.

"Volunteer work is a point in your favor," George observed.

Violet cringed at the suggestion that Ryan had any reason to score points with her dad.

Ryan just looked mildly confused.

"I remember you from last year's drive-through Nativity."

"Oh. The Nativity. Yeah, I was sorry I couldn't help this year," Ryan said. "I'm working different hours so… the time just didn't fit."

Violet remembered the live Nativity, too. Ryan had been dressed as a wise man. He alternated between speeches about how anyone who wanted to be as smart as him only had to pay attention to Jesus and being incredibly silly. He did funky dances and talked to his stuffed camel as though it was in charge. He had so many kids laughing that it left a serious impression on Violet. It was the day she knew she wanted to see Audra's brother a lot more often. And that she wanted him to see her.

"Does work preclude you from helping the church at all?"

"Dad," Violet said, "you just said you know he sings in the choir."

"Mm-hmm. I know a few people in the choir." He said this dismissively.

"Your interrogation is making it so Ryan can't eat," Violet said. "He's hardly been able to take a bite."

"Well, I am paying for the food." He nodded as though giving permission for people – including Ryan – to eat.

Ryan picked up a fork with an appreciative glance at Violet. She hadn't finished her tiny meal when it was time for speeches. Rosie went up and thanked everyone for coming and announced that they would hear from Nate's brother, the groomsman, first.

The groomsman approached the microphone to polite applause. He took his time getting the stand to the right height, then fiddled with his tie. He pulled a stack of notecards from the pocket of his suit coat. He smiled at everyone, then began to flip through and rearrange his cards. Violet could feel a collective groan at the delay. And she selfishly worried it would make people even less receptive to her turn.

The groom's brother eventually began to speak. He referenced a few events from their childhood and how they showed traits necessary for marriage. He'd obviously gotten the same coaching from Rosie that Violet had. None of his stories were funny or particularly profound, but Violet tuned him out mostly because she was going over her own speech in her head. He ended with a joke that he was an expert on everything he'd just said because he'd been married for almost three whole years. That earned a genuine chuckle. Violet didn't join in because she was waiting tensely for her cue.

When Rosie introduced her, Ryan smiled encouragingly and wished her luck. Violet was glad she didn't have her notes. Her hands were so sweaty the paper would have dissolved on her. She tipped the microphone slightly and was relieved when it didn't squeal. Then she dove in.

"Hi, everyone. When Rosie was nine years old, she decided to create her own language. She went around talking gibberish, waiting for the rest of the family to figure it out. My parents thought it was cute." Violet caught Rosie smiling at the memory so it was okay to continue. "I didn't like it. I hated that I didn't know anything she was saying except for one word. I think most of it was pretty inconsistent, but I still remember that siston meant Violet." She pointed at herself and saw many people smiling at where the story was headed. "Every time I heard siston, I knew Rosie was talking about me, and I assumed the worst. Every comment must be an insult, every laugh was aimed at me.

"One day, Rosie offered – in her made-up language – to play a game with me. I thought she was saying that she wanted to watch me lose at it again so I opened up the box and dumped its contents – at least a hundred pieces – over her head. Then I left her to clean it up. Now I was only seven or maybe just eight so I don't remember very well, but I think that was the day she decided that English would be good enough for her.

"I know I learned from the experience how frustrating a failure to communicate can be. Rosie probably learned that her little sister has a temper, but maybe something about communication, too. And I think that she and Nate will eventually get that secret language she wanted as a child. I've seen it with other married couples – my parents and grandparents especially. One of them will say something, and even though it's still English, it's clear that it means something different to them than it does to me. It might be several shared memories communicated in a single word. I want that someday, too."

Violet paused to see Ryan smiling at her. And immediately lost her train of thought. That line had not been in her practice. Looking at Ryan had definitely not been in her notes. Did he think she was talking to him? Her eyes were purposefully avoiding him and landing on a lot of expectant faces. She had to get her speech back on track.

Violet took a deep breath and inhaled the shortest prayer she knew. *Jesus, I trust in you.* The next story came back to her. She described how Rosie had learned patience when she grew mold for a sixth-grade science project and started with really fresh bread. She explained that she was introduced to compromise over and over by maintaining a friendship with a sister who had different opinions on a lot of things.

"There may be some bumps in the road, but Rosie and Nate will have a wonderful journey together. I know this in part because Rosie is the kind of person who is smart enough to learn from her mistakes. Right now, for example, she is learning about forgiveness because she asked her sister to write an awesome speech for her wedding reception, and this is the best I could come up with." Violet walked off the dais hearing a few laughs and applause that was slightly better than polite. She felt she could attribute the lack of enthusiasm more to the guests not being in the mood to sit around listening to speeches than to a poor performance.

When she sat down and Nate was adjusting the microphone for his mom, Ryan said, "And the award for the best speech goes to... Violet."

"You haven't even heard all the speeches yet," she said.

Ryan smiled smugly. "I know what I'm talking about."

Violet felt a little giddy at his approval, and really giddy at finally being done with that speech. Her water glass had been refilled while she was gone. She took a long drink and tried to relax now that the pressure was off.

Both of the mothers gave similarly sappy speeches about how they had great children who would be great together. They were both short. Violet's dad rose from the table for his turn. He didn't appear nervous. Violet didn't know that *she* should have been.

"When Rosie first brought Nate home, I knew he wasn't going to be good enough for my daughter." He paused to give Nate a quiet stare, which garnered a few quiet chuckles. But then he turned and gave the same look to Ryan. That earned louder chuckles. "Naturally, I had to put the young man to the test. I asked many questions, watched his every move, and offered him many chances to prove himself." He said all this facing Nate. Then he turned to Ryan again. More laughs.

Violet chanced a sideways glimpse of Ryan. He seemed to be trying not to react at all, much like she was. Was he also wondering how loud the alarm on the exit was?

Her dad smiled at the other guests before he continued. "After all this time and serious consideration, I still believe he's not good enough. But if Rosie wants to marry someone, Nate is a choice I can live with. He has potential. I think if she works on him for a few years, he'll almost be good enough for her." He ended with a wink at the happy couple, who seemed to think the speech was amusing.

Violet was stunned. Ryan was a friend who was probably regretting this favor about now. And her dad had just implied to a room full of people – many of whom were her extended family – that he was a lot more. She watched him step from the mic, only to quickly step back for one last line. "I'm not sure about the other guy yet," he said.

Violet wanted to hide, but the best she could do was move the event along.

"That was the last speech," she said to Ryan without looking at him. "I need to start the music. I'll be back before we need to, uh... dance." She began her walk to the other end of the growing room. Rosie wanted the speakers set up at the opposite end so anyone who preferred to sit and talk could do so more easily over the music. Violet could hear her explaining how the first dance would work and how the other guests had permission to take tons of pictures and join in on the second song. She could hear but wasn't really listening.

The burning behind her eyes was too distracting. Violet had to get that under control quickly. Then she had to say something to Ryan, something about how she didn't know where her dad got his crazy idea without saying she thought it was a crazy idea. She wouldn't lie to him. But if she was too honest right now, she might have to smile and pretend to be fine for at least an hour before she could go home and cry. She hadn't eaten nearly enough food for that kind of strength.

Violet blinked and tried to focus on the moment. She thought Rosie's orchestrated first dance was over the top, and if she could get her eyes rolling that should keep them from watering. She watched Rosie descend to the dance floor with Nate far enough behind that he didn't step on her dress. They walked to the center of the room and stood hand-in-hand facing Violet. Once they were in position, she was supposed to count to five before she started the song. At three, a few people began to clap uncertainly. As soon as she hit play, Violet hurried around the edge of the room. She wanted to avoid obstructing anyone's view and approach Ryan from the side. It would be better if he didn't see her coming. She failed on the second count.

"Are you okay?" He sounded concerned and somehow far away.

She was no longer in danger of crying, but her eyes must have gotten red from the effort. "Yeah, I'm… I'm…" She was trying to say fine, but the simple word was elusive as darkness clouded her vision.

Suddenly Ryan was holding her elbow with one hand and shoving a plate at her with the other. "Eat the crackers you didn't finish."

Violet obeyed, realizing she'd gotten woozy. Her head cleared, and she refocused on the situation. Now was the time to mention her dad's unfortunate speech. Ryan was distracted by keeping her on her feet. "I'm sorry about my dad," she said. "About him glaring at you during his speech."

"Oh, that's okay. I know it was just part of the performance."

Performance. That made sense when she thought about the speech as a whole. Her dad had never really been that hard on Nate

90

either. He was just doing an overprotective father bit to make the speech entertaining. That didn't explain the intrusive questions before he went on stage, but maybe Ryan forgot about that or thought he was just nosey. "Well, anyway, I just want to make sure you know you don't have to play along with the act," she said. "I know Audra probably tried to suggest some things. You can be honest if anyone comes up and asks about me or anything."

"Violet?"

She forgot for a moment that she was trying not to look at Ryan. Her head turned instinctively at the sound of her name. Her eyes crashed with something amazing, a look that suggested he didn't think the idea was crazy. But it only lasted a second. Maybe it was wishful thinking.

"You should know that Audra may have exaggerated my ability to dance to get you to invite me."

They were supposed to join very soon, and she hadn't even told him what Rosie expected. It wasn't difficult, but... "Watch them," Violet said.

Nate's brother and sister-in-law had just gotten out of their seats. They walked on to the floor holding hands, moved in a small circle near the center, then came together to dance.

"We have to do something like that in about ten seconds," Violet said. "That's all."

Ryan was paying attention. He nodded confidently.

She tried to feel that confidence while she watched for her sister to make eye contact. It was a very fast ten seconds. She noticed Ryan was still holding her arm as he moved to grab her hand instead. His was warm but not sweaty. Their feet traced a similar circle as the previous couple while Violet reminded herself that this was easier than giving a speech. She turned to face Ryan, put her other hand on his shoulder, and still tried to believe it was easier than giving a speech.

And then it was. It might have been something like a waltz

with an extra step for the extra beat. And it might have been nothing like a waltz. Violet only knew that she and Ryan moved naturally together. He took small steps that were easy to follow and not trip over. It was nice.

He began to sing softly with the song. "All I want this year for Christmas…"

It was so much more than nice that Violet had to concentrate on standing straight so she didn't melt right against him. The bride's parents and the groom's parents entered the dance in similar grand style, but Violet completely missed it. She was lost in a very small world for the rest of the song. Unfortunately, no song ever felt shorter. It ended and another the same speed began. Violet had thought it best to add an extra slow song in case anyone was annoyed at having to watch the first one.

Ryan kept moving as though it was the same song. A few other couples began to join them. Not enough that there was any reason to make room for them. Violet was happy to keep dancing. But they had to talk. The longer she stayed quiet, the more likely Ryan might notice that she was swooning all over the place. She caught sight of the couple she meant to ask Ryan about and nodded their direction.

"I met Sofia and Ben in the receiving line," she said. "They said they knew you from the choir."

"Yeah."

Violet wasn't satisfied with one-word confirmation. "Sofia actually said you were responsible for getting her and Ben together."

He sort of grunted. "That's an exaggeration."

Violet frowned at this dismissive answer. Sofia had made it sound like there was a story. If Audra wasn't the only one in her family who played matchmaker, Violet wanted to hear the story. "You weren't… *trying* to get them together?"

The response was a one-syllable laugh, the kind that says the only thing funny was anyone thinking it was funny. "Do you really want to know what happened?"

"Yes."

"Okay. You may have noticed that the choir skews a little, um, old?"

She smiled at the way he said it and nodded. Ryan did stand out as a young face, among other reasons he stood out to her.

"Well, I think it was three or four years ago that a group of us noticed we were the only ones under thirty. We may have been the only ones under forty as well, but... we didn't ask. Anyway, it was me and Ben and Sofia and two other young women. The five of us made a little subset and started meeting for dinner before practice each week."

"Oh, that's nice," Violet said. She thought of the group that gathered for Tichu every Friday now. It was a highlight of her week.

"Yeah, it was." Ryan's emphasis landed on was. "We were a good group of friends for I think at least six months."

"And then?" Violet prompted. He seemed to be pausing a long time before he got to the matchmaking part.

Ryan sighed. "Then I decided to ask Sofia if she'd like to do something without the rest of the group. She told me she'd much rather do something with Ben. I told him he should ask her."

"Oh." Violet understood why Ryan was uncomfortable, but now she wondered why Sofia had made it sound like a lovely story for all involved.

"The two of them didn't need the rest of the group after that, and it got kind of awkward with just me and two women. I'm the only one still in the choir now anyway."

"Oh," Violet said again. She was very curious if some sort of triangle made it awkward, but she wasn't going to ask. She'd heard enough story for the moment.

Ryan suddenly stepped back and spun her around. It was probably his way of changing the subject, but it surprised a smile out of Violet and was just in time for the music to pick up speed. "We can dance more after we find you some food," he said, pulling her towards the buffet table without leaving time for argument.

The caterers had mostly cleared away the lunch, but Violet found a few things she could eat quickly. Ryan appeared relieved on her behalf. Another person was snagging leftover food. It was the guy Rosie had threatened to pair Violet with for the dance. She didn't introduce him that way, but Ryan recognized the connection and commented on the constant throat-clearing as they returned to the dance floor.

They danced further apart than before with more energy. It was impossible to have any real discussion like that. Violet introduced Ryan to a few family members who danced past. None of them asked how long they'd been dating or anything embarrassing. The time zipped by until there was a break for wedding cake.

It was delicious. Ryan said the one she made for his birthday was better, which was sweet. They danced to a few more songs, and then the party began to wind down. Violet told him he could get to the restaurant to relieve Audra. She actually said to make sure Audra wasn't screwing it up, and he appreciated the joke. She had to stay and clean up. He thanked her for the invitation and said he'd had fun. Violet believed him. She believed they were becoming closer friends. But she didn't believe anything beyond that. Yet.

9

Audra said, "Why not?"

Ryan resisted the urge to walk away. She'd only follow him. "Because it's a bad idea."

"She told me she had a good time at the wedding," Audra said. "Now you should just ask her out."

"She had a good time at the wedding because it was a wedding. There was music and cake and... it wasn't because I was there."

Audra leaned against the counter between them. She tipped her head and squinted her eyes and looked thoroughly frustrated with him.

The feeling was mutual.

"So you're not going to ask her?" Audra asked.

"No, I'm not."

"You're saying you want me to continue to arrange times for you to be together?"

"No," Ryan said emphatically, "I am absolutely not saying that."

She brightened and smiled knowingly. "Okay. Got it."

"I don't think you do," he said. He was afraid she was already hatching another plan.

"No, I got it. You *don't* want me to keep helping." She was clearly saying the opposite of what she meant.

Ryan couldn't tell if she was trying to annoy him – in which case continuing the argument would only give her more ammunition – or if she really believed he was doing the same thing.

"Hey, uh… there's a delivery guy at the back door." Ben had stuck his head through the door in the kitchen.

"Thanks," Ryan said, as much for the interruption as the notification. He followed the kid back into the kitchen. By the time he finished accepting and putting away the delivery, a few more customers had arrived to distract Audra.

The dinner hours were less busy than lunch – especially on a Tuesday – but they were down an employee. Ryan and Audra were both moving around more than usual. She didn't bug him about anything that wasn't work-related until they were within a half hour of closing. Ryan was scrubbing a table in the kitchen when Audra burst in.

"Ryan, have you checked your phone?" Her expression said she was worried about something. Or someone.

"No, why?" he asked.

"Grandpa Paul is in the hospital," she said. "They think he had a stroke."

"What!? When?"

"I don't know. This afternoon sometime."

Ryan had pulled out his phone while she was talking. He had several missed calls from his mom and a text from Trevor telling him to call their mom. "Have you talked to mom?"

"Yes. She and Dad are there with Grandma. She said we shouldn't come yet. They won't let anyone else in anyway. But she wants us to be ready for news. Should we kick everyone out so we can close early?"

"Um…" Ryan was still processing the situation. "Let's not do anything crazy until we know more."

"How is it crazy to be worried about Grandpa?"

"I didn't say I wasn't worried," Ryan said.

Ben was the only other person in the kitchen. He seemed uncomfortable. He probably wanted to look as though he wasn't listening to a family conversation. But if they closed early it would affect him, and he couldn't help hearing when he was right there. Plus, he did know Grandma May and Grandpa Paul a little.

Ryan took a step that direction to include him. "We close in fifteen minutes anyway. I doubt we'll get any more orders. All we can do for Grandpa right now is pray. We can do that just as easily with, what, four people in the next room. Let them finish while we clean up. We'll just try not to stay any longer than necessary. Do you know anything about how bad it is?"

Audra shook her head.

"I don't know much about strokes," Ryan said, picking up the scrubber again, "but I believe there's a lot of, um, degrees of severity. I'm not ruling out kicking everyone out if we get news that warrants it."

Ben began to work faster. He seemed to understand that if everyone got kicked out, he was going with them. Ryan was impressed that he wanted to get through his share of work first. Grandma May had hired him right before Ryan took over. He'd had doubts about the kid at first, but all the training effort was beginning to pay off. Grandma knew what she was doing when it came to the restaurant. But Ryan was picturing her less sure of herself with Grandpa in a hospital bed. He kept a string of prayers for both of them in his head while he worked.

They were able to lock up a few minutes before seven as the last customers left. Audra managed to follow them to the door sounding like she wanted an extra minute of friendly chat and not like she wanted to make sure they didn't turn around. She had the mop ready, and Ryan said goodnight to Ben. He and Audra walked out the back door barely after closing time.

"When you get home," she said, "grab Trevor and come over to our side."

Ryan nodded. He understood she wanted to be together while they waited for news.

"We can play Tichu like when I was teaching Violet. It'll keep our minds off it."

Ryan nodded again, even though he knew neither of them believed it would keep their minds off their grandpa. There was room in his head for a smaller concern next to the bigger concern. He knew he liked Audra's idea of being together partly because it included Violet. There would be some comfort in having her near. And that was a terrible thing to admit.

Ryan had been noticing Violet for some time, noticing her as someone who would be great if she wasn't completely off limits. It was bad enough when he messed up his own friendships, he wasn't going to risk his sister's. Audra pushing for it was confusing everything. It was making him think about Violet more than he wanted to. The time together that Audra arranged made Violet seem more and more like his friend as well as Audra's. Keeping her that way was veering into dangerous territory.

But Grandpa Paul mattered more. Ryan didn't hesitate to tell Trevor that Audra wanted them to stay with her for a while.

****

Violet hugged Audra the moment she came through the door. They'd been texting so she knew what was going on. "How are you?" Violet asked. "Hanging in there?"

"Yeah, I guess. I was freaking out when I first heard, but Ryan talked me down." Audra blew out a quick breath, still clearly tense. "All we can do is wait and pray, so we're going to wait and pray."

"And play Tichu?" Violet asked.

Audra smiled nervously. "I doubt I'll be able to concentrate, but I thought it would get my brothers over here without having to admit I wanted them with me in case we get bad news."

Violet understood that had more to do with not wanting to think about bad news than not wanting to admit she loved her brothers. They were a close family. "Trying to do something to pass the time is not a bad idea," she said. "Even if none of us can concentrate."

Audra nodded and moved towards her bedroom to get comfortable. Violet paced the living room and hoped she didn't look too comfortable. She was in her pajamas when she got the news from Audra. When she heard that Audra had invited her brothers over, Violet added a robe. It was December so she was wearing a long-sleeved nightgown that went past her knees. It was hardly indecent. She thought the robe made her look like someone who was expecting company though and would keep Ryan and Trevor from feeling as though they were intruding. But maybe she should have put on real clothes. Had anyone written the etiquette for this exact situation?

There was a knock before Audra emerged. Violet went to open the front door. Ryan was standing behind it with a slightly pained expression. She immediately threw her arms around him and said, "I'm sorry; this is scary," as she let go.

He nodded and said, "Thank you."

Violet stepped back to let him and Trevor inside. Audra had returned to the main room and was already holding the box of Tichu cards.

"You sure you want to play?" Ryan asked.

"Yes." Audra motioned everyone towards the table. "Maybe we'll be so distracted that we'll make stupid mistakes and that will make us laugh. Laughter is good."

Trevor pointed at a chair not opposite him. "If stupid mistakes is your plan, you can be on Violet's team."

The comment made Audra smile, a moment of respite already. Trevor said he would keep score. All three siblings kept their phones on the table to watch for updates. Violet pulled a clip out of her pocket to get her hair out of the way. She caught Ryan watching her with his brow furrowed.

"What?" she asked.

"How do you do that?"

"Do what?"

He shrugged. "I don't know. You have all that, um, hair, and it's like you grab it and stab it and it just stays all nice up on your head."

"Practice," Violet said, feeling self-conscious and trying not to read too much into what might have been more of a puzzle than a compliment.

Ryan smiled at her answer. He didn't actually want a tutorial on pinning up hair.

They were still sorting the first hand when all three phones lit up with what was apparently a group text. Audra read it out loud. "Initial reports suggest the stroke was mild. Grandma is talking to the doctor now. Stay tuned for more details."

There was a collective sigh. Plenty of uncertainty kept them from fully relaxing, but the word mild had injected more optimism in the situation.

Violet placed the cards she wanted to pass on the table. Trevor was ready first. She traded with him and then Audra. When she pushed a card towards Ryan, their fingers briefly collided as he took it. She was reminded of holding his hand on the dance floor. The memory made her squish her lips together to keep from smiling. But then she remembered something more recent and nearly dropped her cards.

She'd hugged him at the door. It was a quick, not-even-a-bit-romantic hug. The stress of the situation made it completely natural. It shouldn't have been anything to worry about. No problem at all. Except that she hadn't hugged Trevor. It hadn't even occurred to her to consider hugging Trevor. Her actions had announced that she thought of the two guys very differently. That was why it might be a problem.

The game progressed in silence. Despite the flub, Violet's thoughts were mostly split between her cards and concern for her friends' family. She tried to keep the game moving and squeezed in a Hail Mary or two for Paul Norman whenever there was a pause for dealing. Everyone made an occasional comment about a good play or something that should have won. It was clear that thoughts were elsewhere.

In the middle of a round, Ryan's phone rang.

"It's Mom," he said, jumping up and turning around as he answered it. He stayed right next to the table. The move was more about concentrating on the call than a bid for privacy.

Violet listened with the others. There wasn't much information from Ryan's side of the conversation as he was mostly accepting information. He confirmed that Audra and Trevor were with him. He said yeah and okay a lot. He said something wasn't a problem and something he would do on Thursday. Audra widened her eyes at Violet to show her impatience with getting all the news relayed.

Ryan's overall body language said he was relaxing. The news must be relatively good. Violet and the others had set their cards down as soon as they knew who was calling. They were ready to listen when he put the phone down.

"Mom said the stroke was pretty mild and might have even been something called a T.I.A. It didn't sound as though she knows what that is any better than I do, but it's something sort of like a stroke with faster recovery. I guess that means it's good if it was that. At any rate, Grandpa's left side was affected. Nothing is paralyzed and they expect him to regain full use, but right now his left arm and leg are sort of weak. She said he can move everything but has to kind of think about it. Um…" Ryan glanced at the ceiling for a second. He seemed to be working to recount everything he'd heard. "He'll

101

have to do some therapy and they're not sure how long yet, but it'll be outpatient. He'll probably be released from the hospital on Thursday, but that's not certain. Visiting is pretty tight. Mom said it'd be better to just wait until he's home. You should call Grandma if you want to try to get to the hospital to find out a good time."

"Is that everything?" Audra said when he seemed to have finished the summary.

"I think so," Ryan said. "But Mom said either of you can call her if you want more details."

"Not necessary," Trevor said. He was already fanning out his cards.

"This is good, right?" Audra said. "I mean, it sucks that Grandpa has a bunch of therapy coming, but it sounds lots better than anything I've been picturing."

"Yeah, it's good." Ryan spoke slowly, still turning over all the news in his head. "Well, it's not *good*. But it sounds like about the best we could have hoped for so... uh, I hope no one thinks I'm callous if I suggest we get back to the game. Grandma asked if I could open for her tomorrow so I need to call it a night as soon as we finish beating you."

Violet shared a quick smile with Ryan over his teasing tone. She didn't even know who was winning, and the way his eyes dared her to argue suggested he didn't either. Trevor hadn't mentioned it, and she thought it seemed inappropriate to ask. Violet studied her hand as she tried to remember what had happened right before the phone call. She was about to ask whose lead it was when Trevor tossed a card out. Apparently, he knew it was his. She shared another smile with Ryan over the eagerness.

The mood lifted somewhat. Audra began to talk about a painting idea her grandpa had been bugging her to try. He wanted her to paint a treehouse in a wooded area where a close inspection showed the treehouse wasn't actually attached to any of the trees. Audra didn't know if she could do that and didn't think treehouses really meshed with her style. But now that he'd gone and gotten sick on her, she felt she'd have to try it for him. She had a lot of description of his request and her thoughts on it. Trevor grumbled about all the talking holding up the game.

Violet glanced at Ryan to see if he was amused that the normal dynamic had returned. He didn't seem to be paying attention. She realized that he was still more somber than usual. While it would have been reasonable to assume he was thinking about his grandfather or the extra task of opening the restaurant in the morning, Violet worried that it had something to do with her. All that smiling over who was winning might have counted as flirting. And after she hugged him, too. She was being really obvious, and he might be wondering when and how he was going to have to let her down easy.

It was Ryan's turn to deal. Trevor and Audra were "discussing" whether or not she'd made a mistake in the last round. Violet was trying really hard not to watch Ryan for signs that he knew she was watching him for any reason. His eyes lifted to her face briefly as he tossed a card her way. She reached across the table to grab the instruction sheet out of the box.

"What are you looking up?" Audra asked.

"Nothing. Just curious," Violet said. She was curious if having somewhere else to direct her eyes would keep her from looking at Ryan. It was a better distraction than she expected. Having learned the game from friends who already knew how to play, Violet had never read the instructions.

"Hey, did you guys know we're supposed to play counter-clockwise?"

"We don't do that," Trevor said.

Audra rolled her eyes at what she thought was an insufficient answer. "We tried to play counter-clockwise the first few times, but it was hard to go backwards and when we realized it was unnecessary, we went with the optional play normally rule."

"We had to explain unnecessary to Audra," Ryan said. "We started a game backwards and rearranged our seats to play clockwise the next round. Then she got it."

"Well, I think I was like eleven when we learned," Audra said. "Since the box says thirteen plus, I was actually quite advanced."

"Quite," Trevor repeated sarcastically.

Violet had kept reading while she listened. "And we're not supposed to deal either? Set the cards in the center and take turns taking one."

"Oh, I forgot about that," Audra said. "That was something else we tried and deemed unnecessary. It was surprisingly complicated to take turns drawing cards. Either we'd be bumping into each other's hands or Trevor would be complaining that it was too slow. And we knocked over the pile."

"Cards are dealt for a reason," Trevor said.

Ryan's tone was less derisive. "Yeah, but I think the idea was to allow a pause to consider the Grand Tichu. That's just as easy to do from separate piles though."

"And faster," Trevor said. "Or it's *usually* faster."

The emphasis indicated a hint, and Violet realized there was a pile of cards in front of her while everyone else had already sorted theirs. She put down the instructions and worked to catch up. The guys never really liked a lot of chatter, and it was probably worse than usual when Ryan was facing an unexpectedly early workday.

The round was fast once Violet stopped holding it up. It ended before she had played much, and she finally learned the score. Ryan and Trevor won after the next round. It wasn't surprising or offensive when they ducked out immediately. They did say thanks for the game and the distraction.

Audra closed the door behind the guys and met Violet's eyes intently. "Okay. I need to talk to Logan in a minute. But first I want to say that I think I finally have an example."

"An example of what?"

"You know how Alison's mom is always talking about finding the good... She likes to talk about how God can bring some good out of any situation. Now I can tell her how my grandpa was in the hospital, and it gave you and Ryan a chance to exchange a few meaningful looks."

Violet didn't know what to say to that. She wasn't super excited to hear Audra talking about meaningful looks that were one-sided and even more noticeable than she'd hoped. But she knew Audra would talk about it as though it meant her plan was going well and leave out any knowledge of Violet's hopes. Mostly, Violet was surprised Audra could spare any thoughts for matchmaking during a family crisis.

"It's not like I planned anything," Audra said. "If I had, then that wouldn't be God working his magic, not that God is magic or... I'm kind of scatterbrained still." Audra shook her head as though that would straighten it. "My point is... I was only thinking that I knew my mom would call Ryan first when there was news so I wanted us to be together so she'd only have to call one of us, and I'd know right away. The fact that you and Ryan got a little extra time together was a bonus I can't take credit for. So are you ready now?"

"Ready for what?"

"To take over," Audra said. A hint of a smile gave away that she knew the answer didn't clarify anything.

Violet smiled back and waited for a real answer.

"I don't have any more matchmaking ideas right now," Audra said. "I tried to get Ryan to take over. That didn't work. I know you guys were texting a bunch to get all the details for the wedding. Can't you just casually ask him to..."

"It wasn't a bunch," Violet said. "We exchanged *a few* texts about logistics. Nothing beyond that." She noticed that Audra's eyes seemed to be scanning the air. She was still trying to finish her suggestion. Maybe she understood to at least some degree that casually suggesting something wasn't that easy. "Ask him to do what?" Violet challenged.

Audra scrunched her eyes at being caught thinking so hard. "I was just realizing that Ryan eats most of his meals, except breakfast, at the restaurant. And sometimes he eats with Mom and Dad on Sundays. A quick bite to eat might not be an enticing offer. I mean, it would be because it was from you, but it wouldn't be... Oh! You could come to the restaurant for dinner one night. It'd be like you were there to see me, but I'm sure Ryan would say hello, and if I just happened to be extra busy he might –"

Violet interrupted before Audra worked out an entire script. "I eat dinner right after working out when I'm kind of sweaty and gross. If I shower first, I'll be in pajamas."

"Well, you could... Saturday! If you come on Saturday, you could come in at lunch."

"You don't work on Saturdays."

"So?" Audra was honestly confused. Her pretense had been forgotten quickly.

"You said I'd come to see you and just happen to..."

"Oh, right. I'll be next door in the morning, which means..." Audra brightened with yet another angle to her idea. "It means you can come and see my paintings, and then we'll go over for lunch together. If I get Logan to come, it'll be like a surprise double date."

Violet had to laugh at how determined Audra was in trying to make something work. "Except," she said, "it'll be nothing like a surprise or a double date. Ryan will be working. He can't just sit down with us. I'd be a rather suspicious third wheel. Plus, it's not a surprise because you've done that exact plan before."

"But not with you and Ryan. And the others were totally grateful for my help. Eventually."

"Yes, totally grateful," Violet repeated sarcastically. Trevor had actually needed Audra's help, but it was unlikely he'd ever admitted it. "But Ryan will know that I know you've done this before. He'll know why I'm there and that I know why I'm there."

"Don't worry about… He'll think I badgered you into coming, just like I'm badgering him about all my plans."

Violet did not like the sound of Ryan being badgered into spending time with her. "It's just not going to work," she said.

Audra sighed. "Okay. I guess it's on me to come up with something all on my own. And someday I will. In the meantime, I'll keep working on Ryan. I think he's grouchy because he's gotten the 'just friends' speech a few times. I mean, it's not like he discusses that sort of thing with me, but I pay attention. I know it happened at least once. And anyway…" Audra held up a finger. She seemed to have tangented off by herself but was back to addressing Violet. "Don't give up on me," she said. "I'll figure this out."

Violet nodded and said, "Okay. Good luck and goodnight."

Audra already had her phone out to talk to Logan. Violet went into her room for the night. She picked up the prayer journal with the pretty cover and thought about opening it. Instead, she folded her hands on the cover and talked to God about a few things on her mind, Ryan being one of them. Violet was convinced she'd tipped her hand, so to speak, and now it was only a matter of time before he felt the need to clarify that he'd only ever be a friend. But despite her relative certainty on a mental level, there was still a feeling of hope that she couldn't shake. That was why she couldn't bring herself to tell Audra it was time to give up. She prayed that if the hope was coming from God that he would inspire Audra with a good idea. And if it wasn't from God that she and Ryan could maintain a friendship after his rejection. And maybe that none of their other friends would find out about it.

10

Ryan pulled his hand back at the threatening look from Grandpa Paul. "Unless you're not done with it?" he said.

"I think I've had enough coffee," Grandpa said. He glanced down and back up, daring Ryan to pick up the mug.

Ryan hesitated one more second before he grabbed the mug – and John's – to take to the kitchen. He did work there, after all, and regularly cleared the table for Grandpa and his friends. It wasn't about treating Grandpa like an invalid, which was what the threatening look was about.

"The boy's just doing his job," Fred said.

"He only thinks you're a little different," John added.

Two of the older guys chuckled at that, and Ryan was happy to see Grandpa Paul crack a smile before he walked through the kitchen door. Grandpa had insisted on coming back to the restaurant his first morning out of the hospital. He looked really good for a guy who'd had a stroke three days ago.

His arm was only slightly affected. Ryan had caught him thinking about picking up his coffee with his left hand before pushing the mug to his right. It seemed he could move the arm okay but it had some weakness. His left leg had a brace on the ankle, and he needed a walker.

Ryan had come in early to visit and had quickly been accused of being there to babysit the different guy. Grandpa had met his physical therapist the previous afternoon. He had tried repeatedly to get her to say when he'd be back to normal. She would only ever say that every patient was different. She wouldn't even give an estimate. Grandpa was displaying his frustration by making 'different' the joke of the day.

They were laughing at something else when Ryan returned from the kitchen.

"And then she said, 'I thought that *was* the flat one.'" Fred shook his head. "I don't know how the girl got to be fourteen and not know a Phillips-head."

"Too many people doing things for her," John observed.

"You're probably right," Fred said. "She is the baby of the family."

Ryan debated about sitting back down. It was nearly ten, when Grandpa and his friends would leave. But it wasn't the time that made him wary. It was the disapproving way they were talking about their grandkids. He claimed the chair anyway, ready to be a source of entertainment if they turned on him.

"At least she's still teachable," Grandpa Paul said. He jabbed a finger at Ryan. "This one thinks he knows more than me."

That didn't take long, Ryan thought. He guessed this was going to be about the menus.

Grandpa Paul paused with the air of someone about to reveal something shocking before he said, "He wants to change the menu."

"What!?" John appeared appropriately shocked.

Fred said, "There's nothing wrong with the menu."

"I'm not changing the food we serve," Ryan said, "just updating the physical menus."

John wrinkled his forehead in confusion.

Fred pointed at a menu and said, "There's nothing wrong with the menus."

"We've been using the same ones for years," Grandpa said. "I haven't heard any complaints."

"It's because we've used them for years that I plan to replace them," Ryan said. The January Café had the same menus so long that many had been lost or damaged over the years. The ones that were left had creases and frayed corners. Because so many of the regulars didn't bother to use them, employees only made sure there was at least one on each table. If a new group actually needed menus, a server might have to grab a few from surrounding tables. Also, a few changes had been written by hand since the menus were printed. Ryan figured that as long as he was going to order more menus, it'd be good to get those changes merged. He didn't go into details to defend the decision because he knew his grandpa knew about the menus after Audra visited him the previous night. There was no way she hadn't already gone into more detail than necessary. She was excited about it.

"I suppose I'll be replaced next," Grandpa said, though he clearly didn't believe that.

"Of course not," Ryan said. "This is a minor update."

"Minor? You should see the elaborate pictures Audra's cooking up."

"That girl has some amazing talent," Fred said, "but I don't think flowers and trees will help anyone decide what to eat."

Ryan silently agreed. He'd asked Audra to design the new menus because he thought she'd have a good eye for fonts that went together and an attractive layout. He thought she understood that it didn't need embellishments when she agreed to come up with something simple and easy to read. But elaborate pictures did not sound simple or easy to read.

"I still don't see why the menus need to be changed," John said.

"Not changed," Ryan said. "Just updated."

"It'll be *different*, won't it?" Grandpa gestured to his walker to remind them of his displeasure with the word.

"Paul, you'll only be different for a month or seven."

John laughed. "He only wanted her to give him an estimate so he could beat it anyway."

"Hey! Goals are good," Grandpa said. He seemed pleased that they knew he wanted to beat an estimate. "Ryan needs goals."

"What?" Ryan's primary goal was keeping the restaurant successful. That should be obvious and laudable, but given the criticism he was getting over a minor change, he wasn't sure he wanted to point that out.

"Oh, did I say goals?" Grandpa said. "I meant a better half."

John and Fred guffawed.

And now Ryan wanted to talk about his goals.

"Audra says she's been working hard to get him fixed up with her roommate, Violet." He explained to his friends in a tone that suggested Audra deserved sympathy for how much she'd been nagging, then Grandpa turned to Ryan. "Violet's a nice girl. You should play along with a setup."

"Do we know Violet?" Fred asked.

"Violet Neuman," Grandpa said. "Chuck's granddaughter."

"He has a few, doesn't he?"

"The youngest. The taller one."

"Oh, right." Fred looked at John, who shook his head.

Fred said, "We still don't know who you're talking about."

"I'll point her out on Sunday."

John nodded approvingly. "A Catholic girl? She got a horn or something? Why are you giving your sister a hard time?"

Ryan glanced around. It was unusual for the place to be completely empty, even at this odd time. If some people wanted to come in for a late breakfast or early lunch, he'd happily jump up to welcome them. The door remained closed.

And the question remained on the table. Three pairs of wrinkly eyes waited for an answer and clearly expected to be amused no matter what it was.

"Why am *I* giving *Audra* a hard time?" Ryan thought if he repeated it, someone would notice the question was backwards.

"Oh, I get it," Fred said.

Grandpa nodded. "I think my grandson needs some wooing advice."

There were still no customers. What was wrong with this town that no one needed a mid-morning snack?

"Good thing he's surrounded by experts," John said.

Fred nodded. All three laughed raucously.

"You say Violet is Audra's roommate?"

Grandpa nodded and Fred said, "That's the perfect place to start. You need to visit your sister more often."

"Exactly," John said. "Gives you a chance to see Violet and a chance for her to see you care about your family."

"Women like a family man," Fred agreed.

"I don't think I really need advice," Ryan said.

"Nonsense." Grandpa Paul snorted and addressed his friends. "Twenty-six years old and he's not even engaged yet."

Ryan's impulse was to correct the mistake, but he knew that was a bad idea.

"He's twenty-*eight*," said a female voice.

Ryan nearly jumped. He hadn't noticed Grandma May standing over his shoulder. He kind of wondered if she'd popped out of the kitchen just to increase the old guys' pity. They were shaking their heads sadly at the correction.

"Flowers. Have you even sent her flowers yet?" Fred asked in a condescending tone.

"What do you guys think about violets for someone named Violet?" John asked the question before Ryan could respond to Fred's, not that he had a response. They began to discuss the new question as though Ryan wasn't even there.

"Tricky," Grandpa said. "She could easily love it or hate it."

"Might depend on whether it's been done already," John said.

Fred tipped his head. "More of a personality thing maybe."

"Or whether or not anyone's teased her about being named after a flower."

"I'd steer clear just in case," Grandpa said.

"Lots of other flowers to choose from," Fred agreed.

John suggested daisies as his wife's favorite.

"May prefers a mixed bouquet," Grandpa said. "Anything with a lot of color."

Ryan looked back, expecting his grandma to confirm that opinion. She was no longer there. Maybe she had come out only to encourage this unsolicited advice.

"Ryan." John said his name seriously, making sure he had full attention before he asked his question. "How are you with words?"

"Words?" Ryan asked.

"Doesn't sound like the kid's mastered them yet," Fred joked.

The laughter was at Ryan's expense yet still not mean-spirited.

"Nothing softens a young lady up like a good love letter," Grandpa said.

"But if the boy isn't capable of a *good* love letter…" Fred let another round of laughter complete his sentence.

"Cliché or trite messages might do more harm than good."

"Yeah, sincere thoughts are what make a lady melt."

"Too early for that, I think."

"He seems reasonably articulate in general," Grandpa said, "but I agree the love letter shouldn't be his first step." He checked to see if Ryan was paying attention. But Ryan wasn't sure he even needed to be there for the so-called advice. He didn't know they were only warming up.

"Oh, we're missing the obvious," John said, pointing towards the kitchen. "Food."

"Of course." Grandpa slapped his forehead. "Should have thought of that. May and I helped make sure all our grandkids know their way around a kitchen."

Fred nodded. "That's the ticket to impressing Violet. Now if we send him over there with food though, it can't look like something he had an employee whip up."

"Right," John said. "Home-cooked."

"This is your move." Grandpa Paul addressed Ryan with frequent glances to make sure his friends were concurring. "The next time you stop by to visit Audra – make up an excuse if you have to – bring something in a covered dish. No dessert, that's a little… predictable."

"It should smell good," Fred added.

"Yeah, if you could bring it still warm, that would help." Grandpa gave a nod to thank Fred for his input, then continued. "You tell Audra and Violet that you found a recipe you wanted to try and wanted their opinions on it, too."

"Oh." John and Fred smiled understandingly.

Ryan was puzzled. Bringing food sounded like a nice gesture, yet the older guys seemed to think it was something amazingly clever.

Grandpa Paul sighed. He appeared disappointed that he was going to have to explain the amazing cleverness. It made Ryan feel as though he was embarrassing him in front of his friends. "Women like to give opinions," Grandpa said, "and they like to be listened to."

"They also enjoy being patronized." Grandma May was back. She'd brought gobs of sarcasm with her as well as Audra, who was at her side looking sort of amused and sort of guilty.

Ryan took that as proof that she'd convinced Grandpa he needed advice regarding Violet instead of what he really needed, which was for people to leave him alone. At least she could see for herself this meddling was not helping.

John and Fred suddenly noticed the Christmas salt and pepper shakers they'd been sitting next to for two weeks while Grandpa rushed into an explanation. "No one suggested anything patronizing. Ryan likes this girl, so he honestly cares about her opinions. He just needs a little help picking which one to ask about."

Grandma May had laughter in her eyes but still managed to shake her head disapprovingly at the backtracking.

"And it was Audra's idea," Grandpa added. "She wouldn't suggest anything that would insult her friend."

Exactly how much was Audra's idea? Grandpa made it sound as though she'd specifically suggested having Ryan bring food. But it had taken a while for the guys to get to that idea. There was no way that bit about flowers had been staged. Ryan didn't remember enough details to know if his grandpa had been waiting for an opportunity to throw in Audra's idea or if he'd been expertly navigating the conversation from the beginning. The possibility made Ryan's head spin.

Grandma must have said something about it being time to go home because Grandpa said, "Let me just walk the guys out."

"Take your time," she answered. "I'll pull the car around to the front to get you."

Ryan stood to push his chair back and give his grandpa some room. He grabbed the walker and slid it closer even though he expected to be yelled at for treating him different.

Instead, Grandpa put a hand on the walker looking more pained at needing the help than getting it. He groaned as he pulled himself to his feet. "I don't know why they couldn't give me a cane instead of a walker," he grumbled. "A walker says 'crippled old guy who can't even walk without help' while a cane says 'distinguished older gentleman in need of minor mobility assistance.'"

"Canes say minor mobility assistance?" Fred asked.

John said, "I didn't know they could talk."

The three friends began a slow walk towards the front door, joking about the education level of canes, while Ryan turned to say goodbye to Grandma May. Though he wondered if he should be worried about the fact that she'd been talking to Audra in the kitchen.

"No need to look wary," she said. "If I was going to do some matchmaking with you and Violet, you'd be together before you had any idea I was involved."

"Wow. You just said something scary as though it was supposed to be reassuring."

She smiled brightly. "Grandmas can do anything."

Apparently, they could twist compliments out of statements that were not intended as compliments.

"Hugs," she said, holding out her arms.

Ryan bent forward to accept a hug from his grandmother, then ducked into the kitchen while she was still hugging Audra. It was time to think about work and being in the kitchen would help. There weren't any Christmas decorations in there.

11

Violet took a deep breath as the door opened. She followed Audra inside, still trying to sort out some expectations in her head. The four guys were in the middle of a round, but they all looked up long enough to give a nod or wave to acknowledge the girls' entrance. Logan was the one seated with his back to the doorway. He turned and moved his hand past all four of them in one big wave. Ryan was his partner. He only had to lift his eyes a little. The blue eyes through the lashes had an unintended puppy dog quality that flustered Violet. It was one more reason she'd never pull off the impossible greeting.

Violet was worried because this was the first time she'd see Ryan since they were waiting for news on his grandfather, when she'd let her guard down with all the smiles and hugs. All the hugs was one, but that was enough. It had been quick and friendly and felt totally natural in the moment. Whenever Violet thought back on it though, which was kind of often, she knew it hadn't felt like when she hugged Audra the same night. And Ryan wasn't there to see that so he didn't know she'd been giving out friendly hugs. Violet was sure he was worried about having to tell her they were just friends or at least watching for signs that he should be worried about that.

But Audra was convinced that Ryan hadn't made any sort of romantic move only because Violet hadn't offered any encouragement. She insisted that Violet needed to appear happier to see Ryan than any of the other guys. Katie and Alison agreed that was probably true and probably a good strategy.

That was why Violet walked into the apartment feeling happy to see Ryan but trying not to look happier than he wanted her to be but also maybe a little happier than she was to see the other guys just in case Audra had any clue what was going on in his head. And then his eyes found hers for a second and she tried to pretend she didn't feel anything at all. There was no way to show the right amount of happy when all she could think was that she wished he felt the same amount of happy she did and wishing didn't do anything. Wishing didn't make an impossible greeting possible.

"How's it going over here?" Audra asked.

"It was looking bad," Logan said, "but Ryan and I just had a three-hundred-point swing so now we have a chance."

Audra nodded approvingly as she picked up his phone to see for herself.

"If Cameron had played a pair when I only had two cards left…" Trevor let his words and blame hang in the air.

Cameron gave an apologetic shrug.

"Is it my lead?" Logan asked.

Trevor sighed audibly. "Yes."

"Good luck to both teams," Alison said. She put an arm around Trevor's shoulders and whispered something in his ear before she waved and headed home.

A few turns passed in silence. Trevor gradually relaxed. He tossed his last card before he looked at Cameron and said, "Sorry about earlier."

Audra met Violet's eyes with more surprise than warranted. It wasn't that surprising, but they both suspected Alison had something to do with the apology, which was kind of interesting. Alison had just said that evening that she'd been enjoying her work a lot more since she started dating Trevor. She said she hadn't realized she was feeling unappreciated until he started hanging around and pointing out all the little things her customers noticed. It seemed she was good for him, too.

There was a fairly even split of points. Ryan glanced back and flashed a quick smile at Violet before he held out his hand for the deck. They occasionally shared some amusement over Logan's compulsion to shuffle no matter whose deal it was. Violet had taken advantage of the shifting when Alison left to stand behind Ryan. She did prefer to watch where she could see his perspective, but she also wanted to hide. Audra had another idea. There was no telling when she might bring it up or how hard she might hint when she did.

"I have an idea," Audra announced.

Ryan paused his dealing, then resumed at a much slower pace. Hopefully, that was because he was giving her time to talk and not because he suspected he was the target of the idea.

After a moment of quiet expectation-building, Audra said, "Christmas is only two weeks away."

"Newsflash," Trevor said, "Christmas is not your idea."

Audra sent him a playful glare. "Two weeks and a day actually and that makes Christmas Eve a Friday. So I was thinking… Christmas Eve Tichu Party!"

Silence met her exclamation. Katie bumped her eyebrows at Violet because she knew it was really a Christmas Eve Tichu/Matchmaking Party. Then she checked for Cameron's reaction. He and the other guys were mostly looking at each other uncertainly. Finally, Ryan said, "What exactly is that?"

"It's awesome. That's what it is." Audra pointed around the room as she began the description. "I already checked with the girls, and I know Violet doesn't have to work and Alison's shop is closed and since Katie is off I know Cameron is off and the restaurant is closed so Ryan is off and I asked Logan so as long as Trevor doesn't have to work…"

Trevor stared at his sister while she motioned impatiently for him to fill in the blank. When he thought he'd dragged it out enough, he said, "I'm off."

"Great! That means all of us can get together early, maybe four-ish, and we'll have dinner together before we play Tichu. Violet and I will host. We can keep the girls' and guys' games separate but in the same room so we can still talk and be Christmasy together."

"You mean be distracted by each other," Trevor said.

"Yes," Audra said. "For the sake of Christmas spirit, you can play one very slow game of Tichu without complaining."

He actually laughed. "Okay, sis. No complaining because it's Christmas. Or Christmas Eve. I admit it sounds like fun. I like the part where you're going to make us dinner."

"Oh, I didn't say *I* was gonna cook."

"You said you and Violet were going to host," Ryan said. "Are you expecting her to do all the work?" He'd finished dealing and sorting his cards.

The guys picked out which ones to pass while Audra stood there grinning like she was waiting for someone to ask her a question. When Trevor began the round with a straight, she tapped Logan on the shoulder.

He glanced up at her with a puzzled expression.

Audra moved her eyes deliberately to Ryan and back while Violet wondered how much Logan knew about all the scheming. Specifically, whether or not he knew that Violet knew about it.

"Oh, right, um... Ryan asked who was doing the cooking for this party."

"We haven't figured out a menu yet," Violet said. She knew Audra planned to arrange it so she and Ryan did the cooking together, but she was trying to stop Audra from saying that in front of everyone.

Audra smiled coyly. "I expect it to be a group effort."

"A group effort?" Trevor shook his head. "I don't think you want eight people in your tiny kitchen."

"I know you don't want me in your kitchen," Cameron added.

"Oh, I know it'll work out somehow." Audra waved a hand

airily and took a few steps towards the door. "We'll let you guys finish this game in peace. Just make sure you all mark Christmas Eve on your calendars."

"Christmas Eve is already on my calendar," Logan said dryly.

Violet was also moving towards the door. She joined in a brief laugh at the quip.

"I mean write Christmas Eve Tichu Party!"

Katie got outside first. Audra turned halfway out the door and whispered to Violet. "You don't have to leave just because I am."

Violet looked over her shoulder even though a short hallway blocked the guys from view. She pushed on Audra's shoulder to hurry her outside. Once the door was closed, she said, "Yes, I do."

It appeared Audra was going to argue but then she said, "Okay. Logan needs a chance to work on Ryan anyway."

Katie laughed at what Violet realized must be a rather startled expression.

"Work on Ryan how?" Violet asked.

"Oh, he knows." Those were the words that came out of Audra's mouth. Her tone added, "And he better do it."

Violet wondered if she should be concerned that Logan was a reluctant participant in whatever Audra wanted. Would he be overly blunt to get it over with? It was too cold to stand around worrying though. They had walked around to the front of the house. Katie continued down the sidewalk as she said, "Thanks for a fun night, ladies. I'll see you next week."

Violet waved before she pulled her coat tighter, waiting for Audra to get the door unlocked.

As they got inside, Audra said, "Okay. Let's think of a codename for Super Fun Christmas Eve Tichu Party with Awesome Matchmaking Opportunities."

****

It felt unusually quiet when the door closed behind Violet.

Quiet and empty. Sometimes the girls stuck around to watch several hands. Other times, like that night, it seemed that they'd barely arrived before they were gone again. Ryan didn't need the distraction of Violet standing over his shoulder or the temptation to talk to her. But he missed those things anyway.

And now he was wondering how much he should worry about this party Audra was planning. She obviously had something in mind that would plant Violet in front of him. While he couldn't help liking the idea of more time with Violet, he could only play along with Audra's schemes so many times before Violet caught on that he wasn't just playing along. What were the odds he was going to ruin her Christmas by forcing her to figure out the nicest way to say what a great friend he was?

"You know it's your turn, right?" Trevor said.

Ryan realized the other guys were staring at him expectantly. He did not know it was his turn. He'd kind of forgotten he was holding cards. "Uh… yeah."

Logan snorted.

"Well, I do now," Ryan said, trying to catch up to what was happening in the game.

"Cameron's ace," Trevor supplied helpfully.

Ryan passed and the round finished quickly once he was paying attention.

Logan recorded the score, then gathered up the cards. "I guess we should talk about this party," he said.

"What party?" Trevor asked.

"Audra's Christmas party."

"Oh, right. Why do we need to talk about that?"

"Well, I'm sure we've all figured out that she's plotting some matchmaking with Ryan and Violet."

Cameron held up a finger. "I actually hadn't figured that out. But it doesn't surprise me after what she tried to do with me and Katie."

"Why do we need to talk about it?" Trevor asked again.

"I'm supposed to be hinting to Ryan that the party will be a good opportunity to try to talk to Violet."

Trevor rolled his eyes.

"Your hinting could use some work," Ryan said.

Logan shrugged. "I don't think you need hints anyway."

Ryan shrugged back. If Logan could tell he didn't need hints, then Violet could, too. This party idea had disaster written all over it.

Logan began to shuffle. "I'm also supposed to remind you that it'll be an opportunity to showcase your cooking skills. That way when Audra suggests you help Violet in the kitchen, you'll know it's a good idea."

Now Ryan rolled his eyes. "Again with the cooking? No one is impressed that I can make food that is edible."

Cameron held up a finger again. "I'm a little impressed. After your grandma let us help make pies, Katie invited me to cook with her. I dropped a lasagna on her oven door. Facedown."

"Dude!" Logan sprayed the cards over the table as he started laughing.

"And she didn't kick you out?" Trevor asked.

"Fortunately, she thought it was funny," Cameron said. "Unfortunately, it was the day before I met her family, and they *all* thought it was funny."

"Ouch," Trevor said.

Ryan winced and hoped he looked a little sympathetic though he was struggling not to laugh.

"Is it my deal?" Logan had the cards back in a neat pile.

Cameron pointed at Trevor, who held out his hand.

Logan apparently hadn't finished his mission from Audra because he returned to the previous subject as Trevor passed out the cards. "Do you need to be reminded that Violet lives there, too, so it would be better to ask her if you need help finding anything while you're in the kitchen?"

"I don't know," Ryan said. "Maybe your hints are too subtle."

"My hints are awesome."

"Do you have any hints about how Audra plans to trap Violet in the kitchen with me?" Ryan asked.

Logan dropped his eyes to the cards he was collecting. "I'm not sure what you mean."

Weird that he was suddenly evasive after being plain about not being involved in a pretense. "I mean I'm having a hard time picturing Audra selling my cooking skills while selling Violet on needing to constantly check on me. She must have some sort of excuse planned."

"Hmm." Logan seemed to consider it, then turned to the other guys as though he needed help.

"Aren't you the one she's been discussing her plans with?" Ryan asked.

"I did my part," he said. "Sort of. Feel free to pretend you don't know why I was musing about you being the best of us guys to offer to help with the party, even though Audra said they were hosting and..." The explanation trailed off as though there was no point in continuing the reason he didn't try to play dumb. And there wasn't.

Ryan was still imagining some contrived situation where Violet had to make sure nothing was going to catch fire because of a faulty circuit or something. Violet wouldn't fall for that. What could Audra possibly come up with? He was annoyed that he found himself wishing his sister had a sneakier imagination.

"Are you still playing?" Trevor asked. He had his cards ready to pass.

Ryan hadn't picked his up yet.

"He's still thinking about how impressed Violet will be when he doesn't drop anything," Logan said.

"Hey! Cheap shot," Cameron said, though he seemed just as amused as the others. He pushed a card towards Ryan. "You seem convinced Violet needs an excuse to hang around. Don't think you have a shot?"

"Don't have a reason to think I do. It seems safer to assume otherwise. With family involved and you guys dating her friends, there's a lot of potential to screw things up."

Cameron nodded understandingly.

It wasn't awesome that he agreed so easily. Ryan knew he was right though. He knew Violet would stop coming over on Fridays to spare everyone the awkwardness. She'd be the one left out if he did anything wrong. That wasn't fair, and he was trying not to let it happen.

"All right," Trevor said. "I might have a reason." He shook his head slightly at the other guys, appeared to be happy to know something they didn't but still not excited to be delaying the game. "When Grandpa had the stroke on Tuesday, Ryan and I went over there while we were waiting for news. Violet immediately threw herself into his arms. Looked like she'd been wanting to do that for a long time."

"That's —"

"No, it's not," Ryan jumped in before Logan could say what he thought it was because whatever he thought was wrong. "No one threw herself anywhere. She gave me a very quick hug because it was a stressful situation. She was worried about Grandpa, too."

"Really?" Trevor said. "She was just going around hugging people because of Grandpa and no other reason?"

"Yeah. Why do you say it like it's hard to believe?"

"I'm just wondering… if that's what it was, then why didn't I get a hug?"

He didn't? Ryan hadn't paid any attention to whether or not Violet hugged Trevor. And he didn't need to pay attention to it now.

The hug was clearly meant to be comforting, not encouraging. Trevor might have convinced Logan and Cameron otherwise.

"She does always stand by you on Fridays," Cameron said.

"To watch the game," Ryan said.

"She could watch from over there." Logan pointed to the side of the room.

"If she wanted to be bored."

"What!? We're not boring."

Ryan smiled at Logan's feigned outrage and responded facetiously. "Of course. When our delightful personalities are on display, we are anything but boring. But when we're silently staring at cards, we're pretty boring. Violet standing here only means she wants to see what's going on."

"Okay," Trevor said. "If you want to believe that, then let's go back to being boring. We're never going to finish this game if no one's looking at the cards."

12

Audra slapped a book onto the coffee table. "None of these recipes say how many people," she said.

Violet looked up, slightly startled and confused. "They don't say how many servings they make?"

"What?" Audra wrinkled her eyes at the question. She'd come home from work with a stack of at least a dozen library books. She'd visited the Tindee library during a break and checked out a good chunk of the cookbook section. Her toes were hooked on the edge of the table with most of the stack in front of her. The two that had apparently gotten her frustrated were tossed to the side.

Violet put a bookmark in the book she was reading and leaned forward to pick up one of Audra's castoffs. Every cookbook estimated the number of servings. She found it listed at the top of each page, right next to the recipe title. Violet was sure she was still the one missing something because there was no way Audra had missed that. She turned the book around and said, "The number of servings is right here."

"Not the number of people it feeds," Audra said. "I'm looking for the number of people needed to make it."

"I'd guess one," Violet said.

"Exactly." Audra picked up the next book but held it in her lap without opening it. "I think it's kind of assumed that one person can make a recipe so I thought I might find some with notes about maybe wanting to have a second person to help."

"Is this for the Christmas Eve Tichu Party?"

"Of course it's for the Christmas Eve Tichu Party." Audra flashed a goofy smile. They hadn't really tried to change the name because for some inexplicable reason, they both found Christmas Eve Tichu Party fun to say.

"Are you setting me up to need to ask Ryan for help?" Violet asked. She'd been trying to get some information about the plan for nearly a week. Audra just kept saying she was still working out the details.

It seemed possible she was finally ready to share. She'd opened the book but closed it again at the question. Her face showed a few moments of indecision before she said, "Okay. I'm actually trying to make sure Ryan needs your help."

"I thought we were hosting."

"We are. But I'm going to get him to do the cooking."

Violet laughed. "You invited him to a party, and now you're going to tell him he has to do all the work."

"First of all, he's my brother so I'm not all that concerned about etiquette. Also, I'm not going to tell him he has to do all the work. I'm just going to explain to him how advantageous it would be for him to cook."

"How is it good for him?"

Audra pushed the book aside and sat forward to have her hands free while she talked. She was all in on discussing her plan now. "Ryan likes to be in charge, and he likes to cook. He's good at those things, too. Guys don't like to pass up an opportunity to show off, especially in front of a girl. When I explain to him that we've chosen a meal that really needs to have two people in the kitchen and how we wouldn't be very good hosts if at least one of us isn't entertaining the guests… he'll see that he needs to volunteer."

128

"You're going to tell him you want to make something complicated, but you need to be entertaining guests so *someone* needs to help me?"

"Yeah. Basically."

"And you don't think he's going to see right through that?" Violet was torn between laughing and being insulted on Ryan's behalf.

"Oh, I know he'll see through it, especially after I've been begging him to ask you out. But he'll still do it because of all the reasons I said earlier. And the whole nice thing. Oh! And didn't you say you were a little nervous about cooking for so many people?"

"Um... sort of. I've helped my mom with a few Thanksgiving dinners, but eight is a bigger group than I've ever planned a meal for."

"See!" Audra threw her hands up in a cheer. "I can use that to work in just a whiff of damsel in distress. There's no way Ryan can say no to that."

Violet tried to smile at the confidence. She was still thinking about the part where Audra said she'd been begging Ryan to ask her out. He hadn't. Did that mean he didn't want to? Was this scheme to get him alone in the kitchen only going to give him the opportunity to say he wasn't interested? Violet did not want to hear that. But if it was the truth? Truth was important.

And then what? If he could say he wasn't interested without her having to confess her disappointment, things might not be terribly awkward. It might still be painful to see him on Fridays. She'd have to avoid him for a while, but not forever. She'd get through it. Audra didn't seem to want to face the possibility of a less than happy ending. She was saying something about how lots of romantic books and movies had a good kitchen scene.

"Working together towards a common goal brings people together," she said. "Creating a meal is a minor, very short-term goal, but it has the advantage of immediate, tangible results. That's what makes it good for a story, and it would be perfect for you and Ryan's story if only we had some momentum going."

"Momentum?" Violet asked.

"Yeah. We had the pies and the decorations and the wedding. Those were pretty close together and especially how you and Ryan were talking leading up to the wedding. I kind of thought my job was over. Remember? I said snowball. But you guys were both like... what snow? Let's just let Audra worry about building a snowman."

Violet chuckled at the exasperated tone coming out of Audra's mouth. And at the words. "You know your analogy went a little off the rails there?"

"Oh, but if I could really get you guys out in the snow... big, white flakes in your dark hair... Ryan would... Anyway, the plan." Audra appeared puzzled. It was more likely she'd gotten herself confused about where she was in describing the plan than the plan itself.

"You might be able to find a two-person recipe – if there is such a thing – easier online," Violet suggested.

"We need a book, but... oh!" Audra's face lit up. "I bet I could search up a type of recipe, then use something similar in one of these books."

"Why do we need a book?"

"It's part of my vision," Audra said. She waved a hand in an arc in front of her. "It'll be not old-fashioned exactly but more... quaint. A real dinner party. I borrowed plates from my mom so we'll actually have eight that match and a long tablecloth so it won't be obvious that we have two tables pushed together. I don't know if I want to buy a few more strings of lights or bring in the ones on the porch, but we'll have cool lighting and you and Ryan will have a book – preferably one of these two here that look the most worn – open on the counter to reference. And I'm... well, I shouldn't tell you everything ahead of time. Let's get back to the momentum."

Violet stared at Audra, who was staring back as though she expected something. "What momentum?" Violet asked.

"Exactly. You haven't gathered up any snow let alone started pushing it around." Audra smiled self-indulgently at her overextended metaphor. Then she seemed to shove it aside. "I got it," she said. "The new menus."

"Are you trying to lose me on purpose?"

"Oh. Sorry. It's all related," Audra said. "I was thinking that you liked the same menu that Ryan did. You should tell him."

"I guess I could mention that tomorrow, but I don't see how that equals momentum. Or anything remotely romantic."

"It won't be if you say it in front of everyone." She shook her head as though Violet had missed something obvious. "This is your excuse to text him. It's very casual but also a point of contact between just the two of you."

"Maybe," Violet said. Audra had been funny about the menus. When Ryan suggested she design a new layout, she knew their grandfather would not be happy about any change so Audra first designed a really fancy one for him to veto. That way he'd feel better about whatever they chose because at least it wasn't the flowery one.

Audra made two designs she actually thought would fit the décor of the restaurant. One was all black and white. It had a chain with square links as a border and block text. Violet liked the other one better. It had a thin red border with perpendicular branches from alternating sides to mark the different sections. Though the text was slightly scripty, she still felt it was easier to read. The two of them had debated the merits of the two menus until Audra said it didn't matter because they'd end up using whichever one Ryan preferred anyway. And that he would like the black and white one. She'd come home playfully miffed when he chose the red one. Then she and Violet had to debate why he was or wasn't wrong.

"Maybe yes," Audra said. "You can thank him for being on your side or for having good taste – even though that's not true – or something. He'll respond, maybe even with a question that gives you another opening. You'll have a little exchange and by the time we have the Christmas Eve Tichu Party, there will be snow all over the place."

"You're not giving up on that snow metaphor, are you?"

"No. It's *cool*." Audra grinned and groaned a little at her own pun.

Violet sat back and reopened her book. "Let me know if you need help with anything other than a snowman."

****

Fred looked at the others as though he knew they wouldn't believe what he was about to say. "She called it a nick."

"A nick?" Grandpa said.

John laughed. "I saw that bumper. Or what's left of it. What would she call a real dent?"

"Let's hope I never find out," Fred said.

The dining room was deserted except for the three old guys. They were as loud as they usually were when they were enjoying themselves, which they usually were. Ryan was listening from behind the counter. The church's new outdoor creche was being hotly debated when he arrived. John thought that a volunteer should put baby Jesus in the manger after the start of each Christmas Mass so people could see him only as they exited. Grandpa Paul thought it would be a logistical nightmare to get a different volunteer each time. Fred didn't like the idea of taking the baby out once he'd been placed the first time. None of them felt strongly about their positions but put effort into pretending they did.

Next, they'd moved on to the current topic. Fred's fiancée, Sheila, had apparently backed her car into a pole. She'd explained to Fred how it was the pole's fault, and that was his favorite part of the story.

132

"You know what this reminds me of?" Grandpa Paul turned and waved Ryan towards the table. "Reminds me of when I was helping my grandson learn to drive. He pulled the car into a parking spot that wasn't actually a parking spot because of a tree. We were at the park, and he was driving on half pavement and half mulch. That evergreen was so close the branches were splayed all across his window and a big fat one scraped all along the door. When he realized what he'd done, he immediately tried to back up to fix it.

"Meanwhile, I was gonna get out to move the branch so it didn't scratch the door again going the other way. I had the door open and one foot on the ground when the car started moving. I cried out, and that's when Ryan started paying attention to what I was doing. He tried to stomp on the brakes, but he panicked and stomped the gas first. When he did slam the brake, I was thrown into my seat, thank goodness, because for a second, I thought he was gonna run over my foot. I might have needed the racing stripes a lot sooner."

Ryan got a good laugh from the story he'd heard many times before. Partly because of the animated way Grandpa told it, and partly because of the knowledge that it wasn't him. "That was Trevor," he said.

"Wait. Was it?" Grandpa narrowed his eyes as he searched his memory. "Now that you mention it, I think it might have been Trevor."

"It was," Audra confirmed. She'd come out of the kitchen tying on an apron at some point during the story.

John and Fred seemed to be laughing just as hard at him getting the wrong name as at the story itself.

"Well, anyhow," Grandpa continued, "it was a good thing there wasn't anyone else around. We were able to leave the car in the middle of the lot while I explained yet again the importance of making sure your passengers are buckled. Because if you do that, you'll also notice if one of them is halfway out of the car."

"Trevor said it was your fault," Audra said, "since he never even put the car in park before you tried to get out."

He scowled at the idea. "I do know the boy was more concerned about what he'd done to the car than what he'd done to me. But I did get to show him how to touch up paint afterwards. We made that car good as new."

Grandma May blew through the kitchen door with a tiny snort and a bag over her shoulder. That was the signal she was ready to leave.

"Looks like quitting time already," Fred observed. He and John got to their feet pretty quickly, though with some exaggerated groans.

Grandpa Paul reached for his racing stripes. Audra had put alternating black and red washi tape along the front posts of the walker and called it racing stripes. The nickname and being able to talk about how his granddaughter decorated it made the walker more palatable for him. Although Ryan suspected he minded it less now that he needed it less. After two weeks, he wasn't using it much at home and seemed to lean on it less when he brought it out.

The old guys walked to the front door discussing how they wouldn't see each other for a few days with the January Café being closed for Christmas. They all had plans with their families. Ryan got a hug from his grandma before she went back through the kitchen to where the car was parked.

As soon as they were alone, Audra clapped her hands together and said, "Christmas Eve Tichu Party!" That was all she said.

"You just like saying that, don't you?"

She smiled. "It's fun. And aren't you excited?"

Ryan was looking forward to the party. But excited was going too far. "It's not until tomorrow," he said.

"I know." Audra let her hands drop, and her expression became less crazed. "I think I have everything we need though.

Violet said you've been trying to get hints." She raised her eyebrows expectantly.

"Sweet potatoes," he said. Audra had gotten him to take her place in the kitchen with Violet, mostly by simply expecting that he'd be willing to cook, though she was planning the menu and being secretive about it with him and Violet. Violet had texted a few ingredients that appeared in their kitchen as hints.

Audra put her hands on her hips. "And?"

Something in her tone suggested he was supposed to be excited now that they were talking about the food.

"Do you want me to guess how you want them prepared?" he asked.

She rolled her eyes. "This is not about sweet potatoes."

That didn't surprise him. Every time she talked about the party, she mentioned that she'd be busy keeping people entertained in the next room or reminded him that Violet would know where all the pans and utensils were kept. Or made suggestions about how he should show appreciation for Violet's help while making it obvious that he could be capable of doing it all on his own. Audra had some intense hopes for her latest matchmaking plan.

Audra didn't wait for a response before she said, "It's about a snowman."

"A what?" Ryan wondered if this was how she got Violet to go along with the party plans. She just talked until Violet was confused and then thanked her for agreeing to help.

"A snowman," Audra repeated. "You and Violet are gathering some snow with all the messages leading up to the Christmas Eve Tichu Party. And then you'll make a snowman."

"I thought we were making sweet potatoes."

Audra had started moving towards the front to greet incoming customers. She turned back just long enough to make a scoffing face at his sarcasm.

Ryan went to the kitchen to check on some lunch prep and the cooks who had started it. He was still thinking about what Audra said, about how he wished she was right, *if* her snowman had anything to do with a new direction for his relationship with Violet. He had doubts though. He had doubts because he had memories of Abby and Monica that had been surfacing after running into Sofia.

Abby and Monica were the two young women he'd continued meeting after Ben and Sofia left the pre-choir group. After a while, he began to consider trying to date one of them. He hadn't felt particularly drawn to either, but they were decent company, and he knew they were Catholic and enjoyed singing so they had a few things in common.

There was one day Monica couldn't make practice, and Ryan still met with Abby for dinner. It had been quieter – Monica was by far the biggest talker of the three – but not awkward at all. At least, it hadn't been awkward until Ryan asked if she had ever wondered how they'd get along without Monica. It had seemed like a casual suggestion but perhaps had been too casual. Rather than a yes or no or even uncomfortable stammering, Abby had looked confused.

She figured it out within a minute and mumbled something about being happy the way things were, though he never saw her or Monica outside practice again. The confusion and subsequent surprise illustrated that Abby had never considered him as a romantic prospect. Having a reason she thought they were incompatible, any reason, would have been less insulting.

Ryan was afraid something similar was happening with Violet. She saw him as Audra's brother and nothing else. But she wasn't stupid. She had to know that Audra was sticking them in the kitchen for some romantic potential. Ryan intended to try to get her talking about that. He'd have to tread carefully to avoid tipping his hand. But if he could get Violet to laugh at or say how ridiculous Audra's ideas were, well, that would be one way to prove he had no chance.

Audra opened the door with a big grin and said, "Happy Christmas Eve Tichu Party!"

Ryan frowned at her. "I'm only coming in if you promise that's the last time you're going to say that."

"Fine. Spoil my fun." She shook her head as she waved him inside.

A curtain of white Christmas lights hung against the back wall. Though it wasn't dark yet, the effect of the lights was already nice. They'd moved the couch and coffee table to make room for an extra-long table with a white tablecloth. It was already set with plates he recognized as his parents' and red napkins. "You've definitely put some effort into the party," he observed.

The apartment had a galley kitchen, enclosed by three walls, and Violet stepped out of it with what seemed like a nervous wave. But maybe it was excitement. Maybe she was trying not to say Happy Christmas Eve Tichu Party. The phrase would somehow be less annoying coming out of her mouth.

"Hey! Why aren't you more festive?" Audra gestured to her sweatshirt. It had a nativity scene with stars that lit up.

"I don't own anything that…" Ryan was trying to say festive, but the word did not want to come out sounding positive. "I put on a green shirt for you," he said instead.

"Well, at least you and Violet will look festive together."

Violet was wearing a red shirt. It was not otherwise Christmasy, though she did have a sprig of holly tucked into her hair where it was pinned up.

"Hi, Violet," he said. "I hope someone has at least told *you* what we're going to be making tonight."

"Yeah. Uh, well, she gave me the list about ten minutes ago," Violet said. "I've been trying to work out a game plan."

Audra put a hand on Ryan's back and tried to shove him towards the kitchen. "Everyone else will be here in an hour and expect to eat an hour after that. That gives you guys two hours to create a fantastic feast."

"Thank you for doing that math for us," Ryan said.

Violet laughed. She moved back into the kitchen as Ryan came that way.

The nearest counter was typically littered with odds and ends. Mail, purses, magazines, sometimes even a newly finished painting drying on top of everything. It was clear now except for two cookbooks and a sheet of paper. That drew Ryan's attention the same time Violet pointed at it.

"Do you want to read the instructions for yourself or do you want me to give you a summary?" she asked.

He did want to see for himself, but he also trusted Violet's take on the situation. If he'd be in the kitchen for two hours, he'd have plenty of time to read it even if he didn't do it right away. "Where do we start?" he said.

"The sweet potatoes will definitely take the longest. They need to be peeled and boiled and mashed before they can be baked." She sounded as though she was seeking his approval despite being the one who knew more.

"Okay." He opened the fridge to look for sweet potatoes.

"Bottom left," she said over his shoulder.

Ryan smiled as he spotted them. Violet knew he was looking for sweet potatoes. She knew what was going on. There was no way she missed the point of this plan to keep the two of them trapped in the kitchen. Was there any chance it got her thinking about him differently? Or had she quickly dismissed the idea?

He closed the fridge and put the potatoes in the sink. Then he turned towards Violet, who was rummaging through a drawer of various cooking utensils. An image of sidling up to ask what she was looking for entered Ryan's head. He ignored it because he knew getting close would have very little to do with helping her search or being heard over the noise of the tools scraping against the bottom of the drawer. He stayed at the sink. Based on the size of the kitchen, he wasn't more than five feet away anyway.

The room got suddenly quiet as Violet's hands stilled. She spoke before he could. "Oh, we don't..." She gestured to a peeler she'd already set on the counter. "I know we have two of those, and I got caught up trying to find the other before I realized it'd be easier if one of us peels and one of us chops."

"Okay," he said. Red was a great color on her.

She opened a different drawer and pulled out a knife and cutting board. "We should have the stronger person do the cutting." She pointed at him with a question in her eyes.

Ryan was grateful that she appeared to be asking if he agreed with that plan and not if he agreed he was the stronger person. While she set to work peeling the first one, he debated with himself about the best way, or at least not the worst way, to start a conversation that could hint at Violet's thoughts on being cornered with him. He noticed that Audra had apparently gone into hiding. Perhaps her obvious move to leave them alone would get a reaction. "Do you know where Audra went?"

She peered into the living room to see for herself that Audra wasn't nearby. "Oh. She probably went into her room. She said she still needed to wrap the party favors."

Of course she had a plausible excuse lined up. But surely that wouldn't take an hour and... Ryan stopped to pay attention to the excuse. "What is she wrapping?"

"She didn't tell me what she got for everyone."

"I thought we all agreed we weren't doing presents."

Violet flashed a cheeky grin. "That's why she's calling them party favors."

He picked up the knife and didn't say anything about the loophole that wasn't. "What do you... Does it bother you that Audra's having you do all the work? I'm guessing the party was her idea."

"Yeah," Violet said. "I mean, it was her idea. But just because I'm doing the cooking doesn't mean she's leaving me all the work. She did the setup and decorations and all the planning." Violet was smiling to herself as she kept her eyes on the flicking blade. "She was so funny trying to pick out recipes. She was kind of mystified at people equating difficult with time-consuming. She was like, 'What's so hard about putting something in the refrigerator for six hours?' And then she was on and on about how the only thing hard about bread was screwing it up. She said, 'Sure it takes a long time, but yeast does all the work.'"

Ryan enjoyed the impression of his sister, mostly because it was clear how much Violet enjoyed it. He smiled at her as he took another peeled potato. He was rinsing and chopping since peeling took longer. The running water gave him a couple seconds to think. Audra had explained to him, more than once actually, that she was looking for recipes that would require working together. Had she been that transparent with her plans when she talked to Violet?

"Audra said people thought bread was difficult?" Ryan said. "Did she say she was looking for difficult recipes?"

"Kind of. The Christmas Eve Ti–" Violet cut herself off with an apologetic glance. "It's a special occasion so we both want to show we put some effort into it."

140

That made sense. Ryan plopped a handful of sweet potato chunks into a pan of water. He faced Violet before he got a little closer to asking what he really wanted to know. "And *I* was drafted to help you because…"

Violet shrugged as though that was obvious. "You have a lot more cooking experience than any of the other guys."

That was kind of obvious. It seemed that Audra had supplied an answer for everything. But as Ryan thought about that, he noticed Violet hadn't quite met his eyes when she said it. Maybe she wasn't repeating Audra. Maybe she was the one who needed an answer for everything. What if Violet knew Audra's hope and didn't want to talk about it with Ryan? He supposed avoidance was mildly better than laughter. Time to give up and read through all the notes on the food.

It appeared Audra's primary way of showing effort was to cut stuff up. Dicing and chopping were prominent steps. "We're putting diced apples on top?" he asked. "No pecans?"

"Apples are also good with cinnamon so we thought it'd be a more original topping." Violet glanced up with some concern. "Does that sound bad to you?"

"Just different," Ryan said. "Maybe we add a little cloves?"

Violet nodded.

"I'm wondering more about the pineapple chicken. Is this right? It says two entire pineapples but only two chicken breasts?"

"Yeah." She sounded as though she didn't understand why he would question it.

"Logan is right. You and Audra do eat a weird amount of fruit."

"Fruit is good."

"It's not weird," Audra said at the same time. She'd appeared at the doorway suddenly, holding a stepladder.

"What are you doing with that?" Ryan asked.

"Don't mind me," she said. "I just have a tiny bit more decorating to do." She smiled sweetly as she unfolded the ladder, then proceeded to stick something that looked suspiciously like mistletoe to the top of the doorway. She climbed down and retreated without a backward glance. She didn't see the dirty look Violet chased her with.

But Ryan saw it. He saw more evidence that Violet wanted Audra to stop shoving him at her. He really needed to stop humoring Audra.

Violet's face softened and reddened before she turned to Ryan and said, "I'm sorry. We can just ignore that."

Ryan nodded. The mistletoe would be easier to ignore than the awful feeling that he wished Audra was right. He'd been wishing she was right all along and couldn't kid himself about that anymore.

****

Once they sat down to eat, Violet was finally able to ignore that mistletoe. There definitely hadn't been any discussion of mistletoe in the planning. She'd been more than startled when Audra hung it up. Ryan had no problem pretending it wasn't there, and their time in the kitchen had been mostly wonderful.

They worked well together. She'd pulled out the colander before he asked where it was and his seasoning was perfect. He'd playfully raised an eyebrow at each measure of fruit and laughed at her insistence that it was just right.

But Violet's eyes kept straying to the mistletoe. Each time, her mind would try to play a scene of what might happen if Ryan pointed out she was standing under it. Nothing would happen. She knew that. He wasn't going to catch her under the mistletoe even if he had any thoughts at all about it being a good idea because she told him to ignore it. She couldn't really kick herself for that though. It had seemed necessary when Audra ambushed her with it. Plus, how much more distracted and awkward would she appear if she hadn't acknowledged it right away? Or if she tried to pretend she didn't know what it was?

The other guests called greetings into the kitchen as they arrived, some of them followed by jabs about not burning the food or taking all night to have it ready. No one mentioned the mistletoe. Violet didn't really expect anyone to tease her and Ryan about working so close to it, though she wouldn't put it past a few of them. Mostly, she expected at least one of the other couples to take advantage of it, which would bring it back to Ryan's attention. She stayed a bit tense the whole time it didn't happen.

The food was on the table a few minutes before the expected time. Audra had set up four chairs on each of the long sides and none on the ends. The place cards that Audra decorated with holly and candy canes put Violet between Ryan and Katie. Audra was opposite her at the other seat that would require kicking or straddling a table leg since one table was longer than the other. Violet tried not to make the awkward arrangement apparent as she scooted in her chair.

"The place looks wonderful," Alison said. "I know I commented on the lights when I came in, but the ribbons and cards... so many nice touches."

Audra smiled modestly. "Thank you."

"Don't compliment her too much," Trevor said. "She'll want to do this all the time."

"Christmas is only once a year," Audra said dryly.

Trevor rolled his eyes at her willful misunderstanding, though Violet was pretty sure he was giving her a hard time without really knowing what he meant either.

The banter continued as everyone ate. Violet was glad to find the food had turned out as tasty as she'd hoped. She and Ryan made a good team in the kitchen, something she didn't say out loud. Audra had decorated the cookies for dessert. She addressed the room as she passed a plate of them around. "Finish up, everyone, so we can sing some carols after dinner."

Violet briefly met Ryan's eyes while the others all talked at once.

"What?"

"Since when are we singing?"

"No."

"She means finish up so we can play Tichu," Trevor said.

Katie sounded confused. "When did the plan change?"

Audra had suggested some caroling when they talked party planning earlier. Ryan had been the only one besides Violet remotely on board with the idea, and he seemed amused that Audra was trying to stir them up with it now.

"We decided *not* to sing, right?" Logan's voice betrayed that he still didn't want to upset Audra even though he was sure about what had been decided.

She glanced at the ceiling but didn't quite roll her eyes. "It's called a joke, people. You'd think as much as you guys give me a hard time about my poker face that you'd be able to tell when I'm serious and when I'm not."

"Well, I was serious," Trevor said as he picked up his plate and moved towards the kitchen. No one doubted he wanted to get to the game.

Alison and Cameron followed him with their plates.

"We will get to sing later," Katie said sympathetically. She had admitted that she enjoyed singing, especially Christmas music, with the whole congregation but didn't want to sing in a group small enough that others could hear her. She was going to midnight Mass where Ryan (with the rest of the choir) was leading caroling an hour beforehand.

Violet acknowledged she was looking forward to that without, she hoped, sounding as mushy as she suddenly felt. Something about Christmas music was making her emotional, something that had to do with the memory of Ryan singing by her ear while they danced.

Katie checked with Ryan that a few of her favorites were on the list before he got up to clear his place. Alison returned and complimented Violet on the meal again. She asked for ingredients in the pineapple chicken. They were still chatting as the guys approached to pull the tables apart.

"I should get the tablecloth out of the way."

Violet jumped back at Audra's weirdly close comment. She was tugging at the tablecloth right at Violet's elbow, which didn't seem like an natural place to start folding it.

The motion did make Violet realize that the table had nearly been cleared. She picked up her plate and Katie's, then reached for the serving bowl still in the middle.

"I'll get that," Logan said, making a move to be helpful.

"No, let Violet clear." Audra's voice dripped with significance as her head turned to the kitchen and back.

Logan pulled his hand back and shrugged at Violet.

She picked up the bowl. A few steps later, Violet realized two things. Ryan was the only one in the kitchen, and several of the others were smiling at Audra stopping Logan from heading that way. Her face flamed at how all her friends seemed to be uniting to give her time with Ryan. It was going to be so embarrassing when Ryan told them to knock it off.

He was washing a pan in the sink and, luckily, the running water probably kept him oblivious to his sister's latest matchmaking move.

Violet opened the dishwasher and searched for ways to rearrange. Surely a few more items could fit. She was aware of Ryan setting the pan down and grabbing the towel near her.

"I think you might have been standing too close to the tree," he said.

Violet turned to him with her brows together. She hadn't been by the tree at all.

"Tinsel in your hair." He reached out as he explained, then drew his hand back slowly, careful not to pull any hairs with it.

For a brief moment, Violet had been tempted to tilt her head into his hand. She wondered if he noticed. He was looking to see if she saw the tinsel that had sparked his comment. And she saw something else, something in his eyes that spoke of tenderness and longing and hope.

"Don't humor Audra," Trevor said as he entered.

His words broke the moment and the eye contact as Ryan turned to figure out what he was talking about. Violet turned, too, but he was talking to Ryan.

"She's going to come in here," Trevor said, "and ask you to go get a keyboard to play some Christmas music between hands."

Audra followed Trevor. "I was kidding," she said. "Why does no one know a joke all of a sudden?"

"I could play a few songs," Ryan said.

Trevor shoved him, apparently recognizing that joke. Then he looked at Violet. "Do we need to help in here before we start the game?"

"That's as full as it's going to get," Violet said, kicking the dishwasher closed, "so we're done in here."

"Good." Trevor led the retreat.

Audra ushered Ryan after him. As soon as his back was turned, she whirled on Violet and whispered, "Did it work?"

Violet backed up to put more space between Audra and the guys before she asked if what worked.

"Did he pull the tinsel out of your hair?"

"He... uh..." Violet paused now that she had a moment to wonder how it got there. This was why Audra had been practically on top of her to grab the tablecloth. "You put tinsel in my hair on purpose?"

"Yes." She looked as though she expected to be congratulated on the brilliant idea.

Violet stared at her. Their friends had been amused when Violet went towards the kitchen because they saw what Audra had done. Fortunately, she didn't feel as though they'd been laughing at her but at Audra, who had evidently gone off the deep end.

"So did it work?" Audra asked again.

Violet thought about Ryan's gentle fingers in her hair and the expression that appeared to reveal feelings beyond friendship. She didn't know how the tinsel was supposed to work, but she might have to admit that Audra wasn't crazy after all. "I think so," she said.

Audra smiled and yelled, "Tichu time!" as she returned to the other room.

Raucous cheering met her shout. It seemed everyone was in a good mood so Violet had no reason to hide hers. She had hope for a future with Ryan and at the moment, it didn't feel foolish. She didn't need any other Christmas presents.

14

Ryan had spent a full week waiting for things to fall apart. And tonight was only going to be the very beginning. Violet wouldn't come over with Audra and the others. Audra would probably make an excuse for her. It would be plausible so the guys would believe it even if Audra was as squirrelly as ever. But when Violet didn't come next week or the one after, the question of who or what she was avoiding would arise. It wouldn't take anyone long to guess it was Ryan's fault.

He knew the exact moment he screwed up. Stupid tinsel. He thought he was being helpful when he pulled the shiny string out of her hair. But he got too close. Or maybe the lighting was too low or the Christmas spirit too high. For whatever reason, his guard dropped, and he imagined kissing her. He had no intention of actually trying, he simply enjoyed the picture for a second. Maybe two seconds. That was all it took. Violet's startled expression told him that she knew what he'd been thinking.

Now she'd find it awkward to be around him, too much chance of risking encouragement. She'd skip visiting the Tichu games. Audra might decide to stay home with her to keep her from feeling left out. Everyone had said they enjoyed the Christmas party, and that they'd be happy for an opportunity to do something like it again. Katie had suggested they pick one Friday for a more casual eight-player game. Even Trevor had been open to doing that once.

That was no longer an option. No one would be mad at him for taking that away. They'd just pity him for failing to make the perfect square of couples. One consolation was that Violet would not be single for long. She was truly amazing. Someone would catch her eye and some other guy by her side would distract the others from…

Ryan chose to stop trying to console himself with an idea that made him want to vomit. He picked up the cards Cameron was dealing and looked across the table to Logan. "How are we doing?"

"Twenty to eighty," Logan repeated the score for the round.

"I mean, overall," Ryan said.

Logan bit back a laugh. "Twenty to eighty," he said. "Did you forget that was the first hand?"

They'd just started a second game so it wasn't the first hand of the night. Ryan had still basically announced that his head was somewhere else. "Oh, right." He didn't look around to see if anyone believed it was a momentary lapse.

"Grandma wanted me to ask if your cooking has improved since she helped you before Thanksgiving." Trevor directed this to Cameron.

Cameron finished dealing in silence. He collected his cards as he asked what would be a good answer if it had not.

"She won't take it personally," Ryan said.

Trevor appeared thoughtful. "I can reiterate how much you enjoyed learning from her though."

Two aces. That would be helpful.

"I guess I have to ask if it's official," Logan said.

Ryan got his hand in order, then looked up as he realized no one had responded to Logan's implied question. It seemed to be aimed at him.

"Is what official?"

"You and Violet?"

That was not a question Ryan expected. "Why are you asking me about Violet?"

Logan raised one shoulder in half a shrug. "The other ladies were apparently making bets on whether or not it would be official by tonight, and I hate it when Audra knows something before I do. She enjoys it too much."

"There's nothing to know," Ryan said. He passed his cards and waited for someone to play something.

Trevor played the one and called for a three, which made Logan wince as all four of them came out of his hand.

Trevor only gloated for a moment before he said, "Is anyone else confused about why Ryan is confused?"

Logan raised his hand. "I am."

"I'm not confused," Ryan said. "I'm annoyed. Everyone thinks these four guys and those four girls can be four neat couples, and you keep putting pressure on Violet to make that happen. Leave her alone." Even Ryan noticed that his tone sounded more angry than annoyed. He tamped it down while the game continued quietly.

Logan recorded the score and began to shuffle for another round. "I'm sorry this seems a little touchy," he said, "but I feel the need to point out something obvious. Violet isn't here."

That *was* obvious. And she wasn't going to be there later either because Ryan had made her uncomfortable.

"True," Trevor said. "I can't speak for anyone else, and definitely not Audra, but I have never given Violet a hard time about this. I'm just confused because I know you like her."

"You're right. Sorry." Ryan was sincere in being contrite. It wasn't fair to accuse the guys of bothering Violet when they were only bothering him. He was frustrated because he'd spent so much time trying to protect her from these insinuations and not enough time protecting her from his own carelessness.

Logan was shuffling even longer than normal. "Are you going to ask for the cards?"

Ryan looked up in time to see Trevor snatch the cards from Logan's hands and set them in front of him. He cut the deck and began to deal without acknowledging that he hadn't known it was his turn.

"I should drop it," Logan said, "but I'm not going to only because it's clear someone here is still thinking about Violet. The reason *I'm* confused is that Audra is convinced that her matchmaking has finally paid off, and Ryan looks like she doesn't know what she's talking about."

"Audra not knowing what she's talking about shouldn't confuse anyone," Trevor said.

Cameron smiled at the quip but didn't laugh. There was a delicate etiquette to letting a guy mock his sister when she was also someone's girlfriend.

It seemed Logan was relying on old information. Audra knew she failed. She'd carefully avoided bringing up Violet all week, except for that time she'd mentioned a game they played and couldn't resist sending Ryan a look of pity mixed with irritation at not making any of her plans work. He'd gone along with all her plans. He'd known the whole time Violet was going to be the one to suffer, and he went along anyway. It might not be possible to feel like a bigger jerk.

"Audra made me promise," Logan said. He was glancing apologetically between Trevor and Ryan.

If anything was confusing about the conversation, this random statement qualified. Ryan guessed that Audra had asked him to be involved in some way. His resistance to dropping a touchy subject made more sense if he was keeping a promise. Ryan imagined that Violet could get him to do things other people couldn't. It was understandable. But it was still interfering with the game.

Or it had been. The topic of Violet was dropped from discussion – though not from Ryan's thoughts – and the next several hands passed quickly and with little chitchat. No one was dealt a fantastic hand. The points accumulated slowly and evenly.

The doorbell startled Ryan. Audra's voice after it did not. "Happy New Year's Eve!"

The other guys looked up to greet her. Ryan was in the middle of dealing, which gave him an excuse to lower his eyes again quickly. He hoped that covered how surprised and happy he was to see Violet with Audra. Katie and Alison were only a few steps behind.

"Did you bring us some sort of... holiday treat?" Logan asked.

"Just me," Audra said as she walked closer and kissed the side of his forehead.

Logan didn't appear disappointed by the answer.

"Is there a traditional New Year's Eve treat?" Audra asked the room at large.

Trevor seemed to be thinking about that.

Ryan shrugged at her.

"What goes with champagne?" Katie asked.

"Oh, right." Logan nodded. "I guess champagne is the traditional thing for some people."

A few murmurs of assent confirmed that was the right answer but not a particularly interesting one.

Audra checked the score on Logan's phone and announced it as she pointed first to Ryan and Logan, then Trevor and Cameron. "610 to 690. Looks like anyone's game."

"Do you mind if we pull up chairs?" Alison asked.

"You're staying?" Cameron looked as though he wanted the words back as soon as they left his mouth.

Fortunately, Alison knew he meant that was unusual and not unwelcome. "He's coming home with me after so..."

"Right. He did mention having plans."

Alison's parents had invited Trevor to their house to ring in the new year. Both of her older sisters were coming with their families. The adults were going to try to have a celebration that didn't wake up the kids.

Trevor and Logan were closest to the extra chairs so they

jumped up to help move one for each of the visitors. Audra accepted a chair but remained standing at Logan's side. The natural pairing put Violet with Ryan as usual. She positioned her chair slightly behind him to his right where he was aware of her but she could see his cards a lot better than he could see her.

Trevor glanced around the room as he picked up his cards again. "No one else plans to stay up until midnight?"

"I'm too old," Ryan said.

"Me, too," added Katie.

"Jack and Alyssa want to stay up, and my parents asked me to keep an eye on them," Logan said. "I'll probably stay up until 12:05."

"Tell them why you don't stay up," Audra said, nodding encouragingly at Violet.

"What?"

"You know, how you were disappointed the first time."

"Oh." Violet laughed lightly at the memory. "I don't think it's why I don't, but... The first time my parents let me stay up until midnight, I was probably six or seven. I remember that when everyone started the countdown – I think some aunts and uncles and cousins were there – I ran over to the window. I have no idea what I thought was going to happen, but I'd heard people talk about watching the new year come in, and I thought there'd be *something* to see."

The others were laughing with her at this childish reasoning.

"It was a real letdown," Violet said, "when, like, all the trees stayed the same. I wish I could remember what I expected."

"Probably nothing specific," Katie said.

Ryan was entertained by the story, too. "I'm picturing new scenery rolling by the window to set the stage for the new year."

"Yes." Violet nodded. "I think I expected something that huge because I remember being hugely disappointed."

"Oh!" Alison said. "Wouldn't it have been cool if it started snowing right at midnight."

153

Violet enjoyed that idea and a couple of other jokes sent her way before the business of Tichu resumed. Ryan marveled at how relaxed and happy she appeared. She must have been able to write off what he thought was a big reveal as some fleeting moment or even a trick of the eye in the dim light. He resolved not to waste this second chance. He would do his best to keep things strictly friendly. Now that Audra had backed off, that should be a lot easier. Yet he didn't exactly feel relieved that she had backed off.

15

Running in the cold didn't make his lungs burn the way it used to. With any luck, that was a sign of being in better shape and not dead nerve cells. Ryan slowed to a walk for the last block. Because it was Saturday, he guessed Violet would be home as he approached the front of the big house. There was no reason for her to happen to come outside so he didn't drag his steps — much — before continuing around to his side entrance.

He stretched and showered before sitting down at the piano. Audra had said they could hear him practicing faintly through the shared wall, which made him think again of Violet being home. Violet liked music, and he'd been playing for years. The practice might only be annoying when he played the same song over and over. Now and then, there was one he couldn't seem to get right. That morning he simply breezed through a few favorites. He grabbed a book and tried to read for a while but felt too restless. He decided to head to work a bit early to chat with his grandparents.

Grandma May was in the kitchen when he came through the back door. She greeted him with a warm smile and a friendly warning. "I don't know if you want to go out there," she said. "Someone brought up the sausage again."

Ryan laughed. Grandpa and his friends liked to debate smoky links versus Italian sausage as though it was a critical policy issue. They all knew each other's opinions yet stated them hotly. The same points were discussed each time. And John always waited until voices began to die down to introduce his preference for patties. That pretty much started it all over. Ryan thought the whole production was entertaining but he'd heard it recently. He chatted with his grandma for a bit first. She still approved of his decision to update the menus.

A burst of laughter tempted him to check on the debate.

Grandma May smiled and shoved him towards the dining room. "Go on. I'll follow you."

As he came through the door, Fred's voice said, "And there he is."

Grandpa Paul turned in his chair to see Ryan, then waved him over. "Come on, son. We have wisdom flying this morning."

A faint snort came from behind him as he moved warily towards the table. The old guys had apparently moved on from the sausage debate and were now talking about Ryan. He doubted that would be as entertaining.

"I think he was smart to wait until after Christmas," Fred said.

"Valentine's Day is practically around the corner." John slapped the table as he raised this important point.

"Valentine's Day, Schmalentine's Day." Fred shook his head. "That one's easy. It's a token holiday where you can do the same thing every year. Right, Paul?"

Grandpa Paul made rather a show of using one hand to cover the other one pointing at Grandma May. "I don't know what you're talking about."

"Uh-huh." Fred turned on the sarcasm. "I'm sure she hasn't noticed getting the same thing fifty-odd times."

Grandma May laughed outright at that. "It shows he knows what kind of chocolate I like," she said. "Nothing wrong with that."

Ryan had caught up to the fact that they were talking about gift-giving and expectations. Maybe they'd moved on again. But then John pointed at him. "Maybe that's why it was such a smart move. He can get in an easy one for Valentine's Day, set things off on the right foot."

"Unless it's too early to know what she likes."

"He can ask Audra." Grandpa tapped his temple.

"Is that wise?" John unnecessarily raised his voice – all these guys spoke as though they were hard of hearing, which they may have been – to address Grandma May over Ryan's shoulder. "What do you think, May? Would she be disappointed if he didn't figure it out for himself?"

"I doubt it," she said. "She's a smart girl. Smart people know accepting help when you need it is a blessing to those who are able to help."

Ryan had figured out that they were still talking about him and him giving gifts to someone and it was all coming back to Violet again. He was most dismayed that his grandmother had walked into this conversation late and still jumped right to Violet. Had Audra brainwashed everyone he knew? Unless someone asked a direct question, Ryan was going to stay silent until they found a new topic.

"You and the younger Miss Neuman an item now?" Fred asked this direct question, but he turned to Grandpa Paul before he looked for an answer. "Do the kids still say item?"

Grandpa shrugged and looked at Ryan.

"No," Ryan said.

Grandpa shrugged at Fred again. "I guess not."

That wasn't the question Ryan was answering. "Violet and I are friends," he said to clarify.

"Oh," Fred said. "They call it *friends* now."

"No, I mean we're only friends."

Grandpa nodded. "Your grandmother is my best friend, too. Nothing only about it."

Ryan struggled for words. His grandpa sounded as though he was agreeing with him while saying something very different. But he'd brought his relationship with Grandma into it. Ryan couldn't say anything that might appear to address that.

"Well…" John pushed himself out of his chair during the lull. "I know I'm not family, but I hope you'll at least consider inviting me to the wedding."

Fred stood up, too, and he said, "He'll cry."

"I might," John conceded.

The guys were getting up to leave. Grandpa reached over and grabbed his walker to escort his friends to the door. He hardly seemed to need it anymore. Ryan wasn't sure if he still carried it around out of habit or because he liked to tell people how his granddaughter had given him racing stripes. Surely he'd told everyone in town about that by now.

Ryan waved to the guys and returned to the kitchen to say goodbye to his grandma. She gave him a hug, then insisted Ben needed a squeeze so he didn't feel left out. The kid looked embarrassed, but he was still smiling after she left.

The lunch rush wasn't as rushy on Saturday as it was on weekdays. Ryan kept busy though. Sometime in the middle of running around, he heard a server tell someone that Audra was out front. He spotted her sitting at the counter the next time he was in the dining room.

"Hey, sis. Can't get enough of this place?"

"I overslept and didn't get much to eat before I went to Next Love," she said, "then I worked up an appetite selling paintings." She held up three fingers.

"You sold three today?"

She didn't nod or say anything, but the gigantic grin confirmed it. Most weeks she sold one or zero. Three was reason to be happy.

"Congrats," he said. "Better be careful you don't sell them faster than you can paint them."

"Little chance of that." Audra's tone was dismissive. She did have a closet full of paintings she'd accumulated years before she started selling any.

"Enjoy your lunch," he said. "I made that."

She pretended to look worried as he walked away. Audra stuck around after the lunch crowd thinned. Her plate had been cleared away, and she was flipping through a magazine. She seemed to be in no hurry to leave. Ryan mostly ignored her until a rogue thought invaded his brain. What if she didn't want to go home because she'd crossed a line with Violet, pushing for a romantic relationship with him? And what if Ryan just couldn't help connecting every thought in his head with Violet?

There was no way he was going to ask Audra about Violet when she'd finally stopped asking him about her. But Audra glanced around a few times, gave the impression she was waiting for things to die down so they could talk. Ryan went behind the counter to face her. "Are you hanging around for a reason?"

She closed the magazine and folded her hands on top of it. "Yes."

When she said nothing else and stared at him expectantly, he said, "And that reason is?"

"I tried to be patient, but I have to ask how much longer you plan to wait."

"Wait for what?"

"Before you ask Violet out."

"Are you kidding me?" Ryan was surprised that he was surprised. "I thought you finally let that go."

"I let it go because it was time for you to take over," Audra said, looking as though it shouldn't need to be said. "And then you didn't."

Ryan just shook his head. What really didn't need to be said was what felt like the five-hundredth no.

"You're going to ask her today then?"

"No. I'm going to leave Violet alone. So should you."

Audra appeared to be waiting a further explanation.

"Violet is happy." She'd looked happy and peaceful at the game the previous night. After being worried he'd screwed up, he knew he needed to try harder to resist Audra's meddling.

Audra sighed. "So you're going to ask her *tomorrow*?"

"No. Why aren't you listening to me?"

"You think I'm not listening? Ryan, all this time I've been trying to get you and Violet together, I've heard everything you've said. I've heard you say that you don't want to bother her, that Violet might be uncomfortable, that my ideas won't work and Violet shouldn't have to put up with me and I should give up. What I have never heard you say is *because I'm not interested in Violet*! I know you. I know that as much as you think you want me to stop, you're not willing to lie to me to make it happen. Will you just admit that you like her?"

"Fine. I like Violet. A lot. She's everything I… and that's why I can't risk her friendship with me or anyone else. I thought I upset her with that tinsel thing and…"

"The tinsel thing was a stroke of genius," Audra interrupted.

That sounded suspiciously like she was taking credit for the tinsel. "What did you do?"

Audra dropped her head and started gently banging it against the counter.

Ryan was puzzled by the display of frustration. He admitted everything. She'd just gotten what she wanted. How could she possibly be the frustrated one?

Audra picked her head up suddenly and fixed him with a seriously determined gaze. "Okay, Ryan," she said. "I'm just going to ask you one question. This is very important so I need to know that you're paying attention."

He nodded reluctantly.

"Violet is my best friend."

That was not a question. "True?" he said.

She rolled her eyes. "We live together, and we talk all the time."

"Also true."

This time she nodded. "Yes. Now... don't you think that if she wanted me to stop trying to get you two together that she would have said something by now?"

"Of course she —"

Audra cut him off with an unintelligible sound and a finger in his face. "I don't want you to answer. I just want you to think about it." She gathered her things and took a few steps before she turned back with a stern look, then continued out the door.

Ryan did think about the question. He'd been about to say that of course Violet had said something. He assumed she'd asked Audra to stop scheming at least as often as he had, and Audra ignored her just like she ignored him. But Audra's expression when she stopped him said that whatever he was about to say was totally wrong.

How was he wrong? Had Violet *not* asked her to stop? Or had Audra been ignoring her the same way she ignored Ryan, by hearing what wasn't said? Ryan tried to think about some of Audra's plans from Violet's perspective. Switching the Tichu teams could have looked like Audra wanted to play with Logan. The Thanksgiving pies and the Christmas decorations had come across as almost spontaneous. Ryan saw through all that though, and Violet was just as smart. He'd only thought she was being more generous regarding the motives of the schemes around her. Having them cook together for the Christmas Eve Tichu Party...

Ryan paused in his pondering to be disgusted at the string of words that had just passed through his head.

That event had been the least subtle ploy. It hadn't been subtle at all. And Violet hadn't refused even after everything else. That moment after dinner when he'd gotten too close, she'd looked startled but not horrified.

Ryan suddenly wanted to talk to Violet more than he usually wanted to talk to her. If there was any chance he was missing something, he didn't want to miss it any longer. He needed to see Violet without wondering how Audra had influenced the situation. He'd still have to tread carefully, keep it friendly unless Violet seemed open to more. He didn't know if he knew how to do that. Audra's question had him thinking he had some hope, but that meant she was already influencing him. Was there no escape?

16

Audra was late. She typically came straight home at noon when she finished at Next Love. Violet finished lunch and talked to her sister for a bit. Rosie was a teacher and had waited a few weeks to do a honeymoon trip while she was on Christmas break. She and Nate had returned the previous day. Violet patiently listened to Rosie's glowing report of sights that were likely more interesting to look at than hear about.

She finished the call and resumed work on a jigsaw puzzle. Audra still wasn't home. Violet wasn't worried, just curious. She suspected Audra would eventually arrive with a sweet story of Logan showing up to take her to lunch. The apartment was too quiet though. Violet got up to play some music from her phone and found a message from Ryan. She carefully set the phone on the counter so she wouldn't drop it while she jumped up and down. Then she picked it up again to reply.

She'd only typed two words before it occurred to her that Audra's absence might have something to do with the message.

A picture popped into Violet's head of Audra sending a message from Ryan's phone, then daring him to think of a polite way to take it back. No. She wouldn't go that far. Would she? Violet quickly typed out the rest of her response just in case. Then she put on some music and returned to her puzzle. It was 1000 pieces, and she'd been working on it a little at a time for several days. She'd had a few days off work so it seemed like a good time to start a project.

The finished scene would be a beach with lots of sand and rocks in the foreground, then water, then sky. The horizon was a different angle than the shoreline and the water had gleaming ripples. It would be a nice picture when finished, but at the moment it was roughly half a nice picture next to a ton of pieces that all seemed to be nothing but different shades of blue.

Audra had a few different ideas on how to make the picture kooky. Violet's favorite was a lake that was frozen but not on the surface. Audra described a layer of ice that had impossibly formed on the bottom of the water and was going to try to paint something like that. Violet would be duly impressed if she pulled it off. All of her work impressed Violet though.

Keys rattled against the front door before Audra let herself in. "Okay, I'm tired of this year already," she said.

Violet laughed. "It's the first day. What did it do to you?"

"Actually, it started out pretty good so I think I'm just cold. Hang on." Audra rushed into her room and came out without her coat and pulling a sweater over her head. She sat next to Violet and surveyed the progress on the puzzle. "I think we've done all the easy parts."

"This one didn't have many easy parts."

"True," Audra said. "And it doesn't have *any* kooky parts."

"Yet." Violet picked up several pieces that seemed to match a patch of sky she was missing. "Do you have the improved picture mapped out in your head already?"

"Yep. It's the first thing I'm going to try tomorrow afternoon."

Violet nodded. She hoped Audra succeeded because if she did, Violet planned to take a picture and have it turned into a puzzle for Audra's birthday, which was coming up in February.

"It'll probably depend on how much progress we make this afternoon, but if I paint tomorrow while you work on the puzzle, which of us do you think will get done first?"

"You might have to ask me that later today," Violet said. "Although… you might have more time to paint than I have to… puzzle anyway."

"Is puzzle a word?"

Violet laughed at the question.

As soon as she thought about what she'd said, Audra laughed, too. "I mean, is it a word the way you said it? Is it a verb?"

"I think so," Violet said with a shrug.

"All right. So you're saying you'll have less time because you've come up with an excuse to leave because my painting bothers you?"

"It still doesn't bother me." Violet got up to retrieve her phone. Audra didn't sound as though she knew where Violet was going to be, but Violet wanted to be clear about her level of involvement, if any. "I, um, I got this text from Ryan." She held the phone in front of Audra.

Audra sucked in a big breath of excitement, then deflated as she read the screen. She said, "I'm sorry."

"Did you tell him to… or trick him somehow to get him to ask me?"

"Why do you think I just apologized?" Audra shook her head in disgust. "I'm not taking credit for that."

"He asked me all on his own?"

"Maybe not exactly."

Violet's spirits sank. She was beginning to think Ryan made a move on his own, one that meant something.

"I was pestering him to do something with you, but I would have come up with something more romantic than taking down Christmas decorations."

"I think it's nice," Violet said. She had fond memories of Ryan looking like he wanted to crush those plastic stars and laughing with her at trying to assemble the manger with a piece missing. It was sweet that he had thought of her to take them down again.

"Yes, it's *nice*." Audra sighed at the word. "It's something that can be interpreted as a friendly favor and not a date. He's still determined to keep the invitation ambiguous."

"But ambiguous means it could be a date, right?"

"It won't be," Audra said. "You'll be putting away all the pretty stuff. It's practically a metaphor for removing any chance of the relationship blooming into romance."

Violet struggled with a response. The opportunity to spend some time with Ryan, the fact that he suggested it without direct prompting, it all seemed very positive to her. But she was confused by Audra's pessimism. For the last two or three months, Audra had been convinced they were going to start dating any time they were in the same room. And now it was hopeless because putting away decorations wasn't romantic enough? "I told him I'd help," she said.

"Yeah. I mean, you might as well see what happens." Audra gave a disinterested shrug. But her eyes gave her away. They practically glowed with anticipation.

That's when Violet realized the pessimism was an act, possibly an attempt to goad her into doing something radical to prove the activity had more potential than any of the earlier attempts. Violet wouldn't be goaded into anything. She did feel less nervous than before they put up the decorations. She was feeling more and more comfortable around Ryan. Maybe this time she could actually...

No. Violet had been thinking she might be brave enough to start the conversation until she pictured herself saying, "Hey, Ryan, let's talk about our feelings."

He'd laugh. He wouldn't laugh *at* her. She just didn't think she could say it without sounding flippant. He'd laugh before he realized she wasn't joking. And then she'd see something. His thoughts were generally a mystery, cloaked by a much better poker face than his sister's. But in the moment he figured out Violet was admitting "feelings," he'd either look happy about that or sorry he didn't share them.

If it was just Ryan, she thought she'd be strong enough to handle either answer. She'd tell him she understood and work on settling for friendship. But it wasn't just Ryan. Violet was pretty sure all of their friends had figured out how she felt about him. They'd *all* feel sorry for her. Was she strong enough to risk that much pity?

****

Ryan leaned against the counter as he stared out the front window. Violet would be there any minute. She went home to change into more comfortable clothes after church, while he got held up by a very chatty choir member. He'd thought Violet might beat him to the restaurant after that. When she wasn't there, he climbed up and pulled the big Christmas tree box out of the ceiling. She still wasn't there so he opened the cabinet in the office and figured out which boxes had room for decorations.

No sign of Violet. He wanted to wait for her, but if she found him standing there, it might look as though he was waiting for her to do all the work. Ryan pushed himself off the counter and grabbed a tray to collect all the Christmasy salt and pepper shakers. Something about the pairs reminded him of dancing at Rosie's wedding. He sang that song as he worked. He was picking up a set from a table at the front when he spotted Violet by the door. She was smiling at him, which made the tray wobble on his hand.

He set it on the table to be faster about letting her in while he wondered if he had missed a knock or if she'd just arrived.

"Hi," she said cheerfully as she entered. "Do you sing to the condiments often?"

Apparently, she'd been watching at least a few seconds before he noticed. She seemed entertained. He said, "They like it."

Violet laughed and wiggled out of her coat. She was wearing the same red sweater she'd been wearing at the Christmas party. It looked incredible on her. Again. "You look nice," he said. He couldn't risk a stronger compliment until he wrapped his head

167

around how to ask if she saw something between them while sounding as though it'd be perfectly fine if she didn't. It wouldn't be fine. It would hurt. He needed to figure out her answer and not ask if she would feel bad giving it.

"Thanks. Where should I start?" Her eyes widened as she waited his instructions.

It seemed she expected to be sent to work somewhere else. Was she more interested in putting away decorations than in spending time with him? He believed she'd wanted to help get them out. She was genuinely delighted by the trimmings. But putting it all away was going to be boring. If that was more interesting, he had no chance. No chance at all. "Maybe you can swap out the menu holders while I finish the salt and pepper. Then we'll tackle the tree together."

She nodded, which meant she didn't hate the idea of being near the tree at the same time. That was a long way from answering the question. There'd be time to get to that.

"The regular holders are in the box by the office door."

"Got it." She hung her coat on the back of a chair and walked purposefully towards the office.

Ryan had no doubts she could complete the task without further input. It was a good feeling, though it briefly made him wish he felt the same about a few of his employees.

Though they weren't working side by side, the dining room was so quiet they could talk across the space. Violet told him some about her sister's recent honeymoon. She amused him with how *un*surprised she was that the trip had been pleasant. She went right from that to a few serious comments about the homily they'd heard earlier.

The respective jobs finished at nearly the same time. Ryan patted himself on the back for getting his pace right as he gathered the appropriate boxes in front of the tree.

Violet looked the tree up and down as she joined him. "We did a good job," she said.

He silently agreed. Every time he'd looked at the tree over the last few weeks, he'd remembered how much he enjoyed her help. She sounded slightly wistful. Was there any chance she was also wishing the memory was the start of many like it? There was no way to read her mind.

Her eyes turned towards him with a hint of question. There was something in the way she looked at him, something hopeful. That couldn't be his imagination.

"Should I hand things to you to put away or what?"

Or maybe that was the only question on her mind, and she hoped they could get on with it. Ryan refocused on the job at hand. He gave her the box for the bulbs and began to pull off bits of tinsel. They stripped the ornaments from the tree in a mostly companionable silence. Except there were a few times when they reached for the same branch or one leaned in front of the other. Violet was overly apologetic about almost touching. That could be interpreted as being nervous, which could be good. Or it could mean she didn't want Ryan to think she got close on purpose. Obviously, that was less good.

He stepped back to give her room to unwind the lights.

"Do you think we should booby trap these by putting the stars back on before we tuck them in the box?" Her eyes flashed with mischief.

Ryan couldn't resist a smile, but he said, "Considering that I'm probably going to be the one to get them out next, I have to say that's a bad idea."

She smiled back at the expected response. "Hey. Did you ever ask your grandma if they gave her trouble?"

"Yeah. She looked at me like she didn't know what I was talking about. Then suggested I was clumsy."

"Oh." Violet frowned. "Me, too, I guess."

"That's how I knew she was wrong," Ryan said. Violet did everything with an athletic grace. If she couldn't keep the stars on the lights, there was something wrong with the stars.

She coiled the end of the string, without booby-trapping it, and set it in the box. She left him to take apart the tree by himself while she started collecting other decorative items. By the time he got the big box wrestled back into storage, Violet had made a lot of progress. The red chairs by the counter and other red accents were looking normal again with less Christmas red to accentuate them.

Violet was on a stepstool near the kitchen door as he came through it. She did not appear remotely in danger of falling. Yet the sight somehow conjured an image of her having a sudden balance problem and dropping into his arms like a scene from a bad romcom.

Violet would never fake a fall. Ryan found himself picturing it anyway. She was only two steps off the ground. She could land a foot sideways on the lower one and tip right towards him. He wouldn't mind catching her, wouldn't mind taking a few extra seconds to let her regain her stability before he let go. He'd have to hold on long enough to be absolutely sure she was steady. To say that wouldn't be a chore was an understatement of an understatement.

Violet hopped lithely off the stool holding the wreath she'd taken off the wall. Ryan realized he'd physically moved forward while his mind was going places it shouldn't. There was barely two feet between them. Violet's eyes moved to the wreath and back as though she thought he'd arrived to take it from her. But she didn't seem in a hurry to hand it over, maybe not in a hurry to back up either.

Ryan's fingers itched with a desire to reach for her. He wanted to kiss her and got the feeling she would let him. But they had to talk first in case he was wrong. They had to talk, and he couldn't process what to say.

A growl that clearly protested a lack of food came from Violet's stomach. She twirled the wreath in her hands to relax the moment.

"I, uh, I think that means we should keep working so I can get home for lunch."

"No, we…" Ryan glanced around. Unless he was missing something, a few snowflakes on the ceiling were all that remained. "We're almost done, but if you're hungry we should take a break." It was nearly two o'clock. Of course she was hungry. He kicked himself for not recognizing that need sooner. At least he knew what she liked. "We have a whole kitchen of food. I'll get you a pile of fruit."

She laughed at the teasing tone of his words but followed him as she said, "A pile of fruit sounds delicious." She found a box with room for the wreath, then took down those snowflakes before she came to the table to watch him cut up some pineapple, strawberries and bananas.

"I think I'll warm up some shredded beef to make myself a sandwich," Ryan said. "Do you want one, too?"

"No, thanks. This'll be enough for me."

"You sure?"

"I'm eating dinner with my parents," Violet said. "Best not to stuff myself too much now."

He nodded, but he gave her a larger share of the fruit. "I could put it in a bowl, but then it would be a bowl of fruit and not a pile."

She smiled as she took the plate. "Nice presentation."

He encouraged her to start eating while he made his sandwich. She ate slowly, and they finished around the same time. She told him he was a good cook as she put her fork down. He could tell her appreciation was sincere though her compliment was joking. The mood was light while they ate, comfortable.

They only had to get all the boxes into the cabinet to be finished. She said she'd see him soon and left. She left before he could ask how she would see him and how often she wanted to. Ryan locked the door behind her and watched her walk towards her car. She glanced back just before she disappeared inside it.

There was something slightly sad in that glance. It made him admit that what he'd just thought was not true. He could have asked. He simply hadn't had the guts. He jogged towards the back door, grabbing his coat on the way. Maybe he could catch up to her before she got inside the house.

17

Violet parked her car in front of the old Founder's Mansion where she lived. She shut it off but didn't immediately get out. Audra was going to ask for details. Violet would have to confess that nothing happened. At least, nothing that changed anything.

She'd enjoyed the time with Ryan, loved seeing him so capable in his familiar environment, laughed at him pretending to sing to Christmas tree branches, savored the conversation around the work and food. And there had been a few moments that sizzled with tension, a few moments that convinced her more than ever that romance was barely beneath the surface.

Each time, the words, "Hey, Ryan, we need to talk about our feelings," nearly popped out of her mouth. It wouldn't matter if that was a stupid way to say it. It would only matter that she said something. But she hadn't said it.

Both hands gripped her steering wheel and squeezed out some frustration. Then she opened her door to make her way up to the apartment where Audra was painting a pretty picture and waiting in her plastic cocoon to pounce on Violet's failure. She heard a car on the street behind her.

It occurred to her that Ryan might not have had anything else to do at the restaurant about the same time a door slammed and his voice called, "Violet! Wait a sec!"

She turned around in time to see Ryan turn around as well.

He opened his passenger door and pulled out a coat, which he put on as he walked quickly to where she waited.

"Violet, I… Can I ask you a question?"

Something in his eyes, something hopeful yet vulnerable, told her she was going to like his question. She nodded quickly.

He drew a hat from his pocket, the one with the pompom, and yanked it on his head. He stuffed his hands in the pockets.

Violet honestly couldn't tell if he was cold or stalling. Her heart was beating too fast to even judge how many seconds had passed.

"There's been… I think there's been times lately when it seemed like… it felt like… it feels like there's something between us that's more than friendship. And I don't know if it's just me. I don't know how to tell if it's just me so I have to ask you. Do you see me as only a friend?"

She'd been so sure this was a good question that Violet was practically nodding the moment he started talking. But his choice of words actually made no the right answer, and she had a bit of trouble making her neck move the other way.

Ryan looked relieved though. She must have done it right. His lips twitched against a smile. He didn't say anything else, kind of seemed to expect her to say something.

"I… don't know what to say," she admitted.

"Just tell me I'm not imagining sparks."

"You're not." She swallowed hard. No one's imagination was that good.

Ryan shifted his weight. He looked past her and appeared to be making up his mind about something. "In that case," he said, "I think I want to ask another question." His eyes dropped to her mouth briefly.

Violet mashed her lips together to prevent a goofy smile. Then she tried to relax them because she knew he was going to ask if he could kiss her. Or that had better be what he was going to ask.

Anything else would be disappointing. "Okay," she said.

He took a step forward as his hands came out of his pockets. His fingers brushed against the side of her cheek. They were very warm, which might have answered the question about the hat if Violet had been thinking about any other question. "Can I... kiss you?"

Violet tried to say yes. Or okay. Or maybe go ahead. Her throat held too much emotion. She only nodded.

The sides of his mouth lifted. It was clear he appreciated how eagerly she nodded before Violet closed her eyes and felt their lips meet. If any part of her was cold, it wasn't anymore. She wasn't even aware it was January. She grabbed the front of his jacket. When he leaned back, he was looking over her shoulder again.

Violet realized he was worried about Audra looking out the window. Or more likely, he was worried about her coming out to cheer them on. "She's painting today," Violet reminded him, "so she's probably not paying attention to anything else."

Ryan brought his eyes back to hers. "Are you inviting me to do that again?"

A nervous laugh escaped and the tension of the moment went with it. "That's not exactly what I meant," she said. "But, um... okay."

He didn't need a second invitation, unless her okay counted as the second one. He kissed her again, chastely but still enthusiastically, then stepped back. "I know you have plans with your parents, but we need to talk more soon."

"I do. And, yes, we do."

"Glad that's settled," he said, then laughed. It wasn't because anything was funny but because he was simply too happy not to laugh.

Violet understood because she was biting the side of her lip against a similar feeling. "Yeah, um... we'll talk."

Ryan moved towards the side and waved before he went around the corner to his door.

Violet waved back. She remembered it was below freezing as soon as she lost sight of him. She unlocked her door bursting with happiness. She knew she walked in with the worst poker face ever. She knew it before Audra set down her paintbrush, threw both hands in the air and shouted, "It's about time!"

****

"Do I get to tell them tonight?" Audra asked.

Violet sighed. "It's not really a secret or anything."

"So I *can* tell them?"

"I never said you couldn't," Violet said. "I just didn't want you to say it like a big announcement."

"It is big news to me. I worked *hard* to get you guys together."

Violet found the overdramatization amusing. "I'm not sure I'd call a lot of hinting and suggesting hard work."

"Really?" Audra was holding the box of Tichu cards because they were expecting Katie and Alison. The box made a smacking sound on the table as she dropped it, apparently just to punctuate her reaction. "At any time in the last, like, two months, I could have said, 'Stop worrying. He really likes you.' Do you know how hard it was to *not* say that? It was on the tip of my tongue every time we talked about Ryan."

"But you couldn't say that because you didn't know it."

"Oh, I knew."

"Like you *knew* I liked Logan?"

Audra waved a hand dismissively. "That was different. Logan turned my brain to mush so I wasn't seeing clearly. Once we were straightened out, I could see what was happening between you and Ryan. Trying to get either of you to see it... I maintain that was hard work."

176

"I maintain that you didn't really know how Ryan felt because he never told you."

"He said it by not saying it."

"He said it by not saying it?" Violet repeated, laughing skeptically.

"Yes." Audra responded to the laugh with defiance. "Every time I tried to set him up or pushed him to ask you out, he was only ever worried about how you were going to feel about it. Putting someone else's needs before your own, that's the definition of love."

"But that doesn't just mean love love," Violet said. "That's what Christian love is all about. Thinking about me only proved he's a good guy, not that he's interested in me." Violet knew she spoke the truth, but she still really liked the idea of Ryan trying to protect her feelings.

"Thank you for proving my point," Audra said.

"What? How did I prove your point by contradicting it?"

"I knew Ryan liked you because of how he said what he said when he didn't say he liked you. Just like you just said he was a good guy while your eyes got all sappy like, 'Oh, he's an amazing guy.'" Audra shook her head, a bit disgusted that anyone would think that about her brother. "Trust me. I could tell he wasn't caring about you in a love your neighbor sort of way. Although – ha! You are literally his neighbor so that's funny."

Violet began to move towards the door, grateful that a knock was putting an end to the conversation she wasn't going to win. "Please just try not to make it a big deal."

Audra wiggled her eyebrows playfully. She wasn't making any promises.

Violet wasn't overly worried about her friends teasing her. In fact, if she was really honest with herself, she wondered if she was making it a big deal by telling Audra not to make it a big deal only because she couldn't stop herself from talking about Ryan. She opened the front door wondering which friend had arrived and found both of them. "Hi. Come on in," she said. "Did you guys come together?"

Alison shook her head.

"Just happened to park at the same time and met on the sidewalk." Katie glanced around as she took off her coat. "Looks different without the Christmas stuff."

"Yeah," Audra said. "Sadder."

The ladies nodded commiseration with what they perceived as general post-holiday letdown. Violet knew part of Audra's disappointment was that Logan hadn't proposed on either of those holidays. If there wasn't a development on Valentine's Day, she was likely to take matters into her own hands. And Logan might never hear the end of that.

Audra took the lid off the Tichu box. "Random teams?" she asked.

There was only nodding and agreement. Katie, especially, had gotten good fast and made it no longer necessary to split the newer players.

Audra pulled out two sixes and two jacks, the first matching cards she found, mixed them and passed them out to assign teams. Violet and Katie got jacks and took opposite seats at the table.

The first two rounds passed with chitchat about what everyone had been up to during the week. Katie had nothing to report. Audra paused the game briefly to show off her latest painting. The ice under the water had come out perfectly. The scene projected shivers, yet it was impossible to tell at first glance that anything was wrong. Alison smiled when she saw it. Katie pointed out the ripple that gave it away.

Alison had found a unique old desk at an estate sale she was excited to restore. Violet stuck to talking about all the pictures parents had been sharing of their little dancers in Christmas costumes. It was really hard not to say anything about how she'd spent most of her free time talking to Ryan. She didn't know if she could talk and not gush.

Alison was keeping score. "120 to 80," she said as she picked up the cards to deal another hand.

Katie nodded encouragingly at Violet. They could easily make that up.

"I know the guys are fixated on Tichu," Audra said, "but I wouldn't mind if you all wanted to play a different game now and then."

"You do have several on the shelf that look interesting." Katie gestured that direction.

"I'm happy with Tichu tonight since I already got in more games than usual this week." Audra sent a cheeky grin at Violet. She'd gotten in extra games because Violet and Ryan wanted a third player for a few. Logan had joined once, too.

The conspiratorial nature of the smile wasn't lost on anyone in the room.

"Oh, let me guess," Katie said. "You got Ryan over here for a game, then conveniently had Logan call you to interrupt so Violet and Ryan would be stuck waiting for you. They finally admitted some attraction when you left them alone." She smirked at Violet, who was sure her own expression confirmed that *something* good had happened with Ryan.

"No," Audra said, "but keep guessing. This'll be fun." She rubbed her hands together.

Violet had doubts about the level of fun.

"You invited Ryan for a game every night this week," Katie said, "and Violet figured out on about the fifth time that he agreed to come the moment you said she wanted him to."

"Nope. Guess again."

"I got it," Alison said. "You brought Ryan over here to teach Violet a new game where he had to stand behind her and show her exactly how to hold the pieces."

"Uh, we don't have that game," Audra said. She looked as though she wanted to say something else but couldn't get it out before she and Katie and Alison exploded with laughter.

Violet was right about the guessing game being not that funny, yet the laughter was too contagious not to join in a little. "Are you guys done?" she asked, trying to sound disapproving through her smile.

"Come on," Audra said. "We're just happy you finally saw it."

"What's with the finally?" Violet asked. She hadn't told anyone how long she'd carried a torch, as some might say, and Audra only knew about it for the couple of months she'd suspected she might have a chance. There was nothing wrong with wanting to be sure before she risked disrupting the group, especially after Audra scared her with some miscommunication. Violet had gotten a glimpse of being left out. But she had to admit she'd been nervous to say anything even once she thought Ryan would be happy about it. "Okay. Maybe Audra could be a little impatient since you've been talking to Ryan so much. But you two," she pointed from Katie to Alison, "didn't know that... that Ryan... you didn't know it would work out."

"You're right." Katie grew more serious. "It's not fair to act like you were blind for not seeing what was mostly wishful thinking on my part. You guys are the best friends I've had since high school, and I knew you liked him. So if he started dating someone else, I'd want to keep her as an outsider, which would be wrong. And if you... found someone else... I was afraid you'd want to spend all your time with him. I've had selfish reasons for... hoping you and Ryan would work out."

Silence fell. The admission of weakness proved there was a connection that went beyond passing time with a game. Violet appreciated wanting to protect that. It was a primary reason for her trepidation.

All four women were ignoring the piles of cards in front of

them. Alison gathered hers without looking at them. She tapped the bunch on the table with a guilty expression before she said, "Well, I sort of knew."

Audra raised an inquisitive eyebrow at her.

"Uh… Trevor said something a few weeks ago about Ryan not thinking he had a shot with Violet, which I interpreted as him wanting a shot. But Audra had been so adamant about not telling Trevor how Violet felt that it didn't seem right to… I thought I should keep what he said to myself, too."

That sounded reasonable and fair and mature and Violet still wished Alison had told her. Hearing it now made her feel that using the word finally might be justified.

"So do you guys want to know what actually got them talking?" Audra said.

Alison said, "Yes."

Katie's voice was a quick echo.

"It wasn't the games," Audra said. "That was just them wanting to spend time together after they started talking. I told Ryan he was on his own, that he had to ask Violet out for real. And you know what he did? Wait until you hear about the huge, romantic overture. He pulled out all the stops for an amazing and unforgettable…" Audra couldn't finish because she was cracking herself up with the over-the-top sarcasm.

Violet rolled her eyes while the others giggled in anticipation of the opposite of Audra's buildup.

"You tell them," Audra said.

"He asked me to help him take down the Christmas decorations at the January Café."

Katie tipped her head as she thought about that.

Alison said, "Aw."

"What!?" Audra's eyes bugged out. "What do you mean aw? There is nothing sweet about hiding all the pretty stuff as unpaid labor."

"But she helped him put the decorations up," Alison said, "so there's a slight connection already… with memories."

"Yeah, and the January Café is…" Katie paused to search for the words she wanted. "That's his turf. He trusted Violet to invade his space. That's a little romantic."

"Thank you for, I think, being on my side," Violet said. "Though I don't know if anyone has ever used the words invade and romantic in the same breath before."

Katie gave a slight laugh and shrug.

Congratulations were expressed on the new relationship, finally, and the women decided to remember they were playing a game. Violet was able to focus better once she was no longer wondering how her news would come out. She and Katie pulled ahead but ended up losing in a big swing at the end. There was a brief discussion about something Alison might have done wrong, not to assign blame but because she asked and wanted to learn. When they got up to visit the guys, it didn't feel any different than previous weeks.

Or it didn't feel much different. The nervous excitement at going to see Ryan was replaced by a happy excitement. The winter weather had dropped snow early in the week before the temperature got enough above freezing that most of it melted. There was only a stripe along the edge of the sidewalk where Ryan had shoveled it. Violet smiled to remember how she'd passed him with the shovel on her way to work. He'd playfully yelled at her for being on time because he'd hoped to have the whole path clear before she left.

Audra rang the doorbell with one hand as she reached for the knob with the other. Violet gave in to the impulse to push the button as she entered. She heard it ring two more times behind her as well.

"I can't believe you got everyone doing it now," Trevor said to Audra. He managed to keep his tone stern, but a lot of quivering around his mouth gave away how hard he was fighting a smile.

"It means hello," Audra said.

182

Violet's eyes took in the very different backs on the cards at the same time Alison said, "Wait. What are you guys playing?"

"Tichu," Ryan said.

"Sort of," Logan added.

The ladies spread out to stand behind their respective guys to see the fronts of the cards.

Violet saw standard suits in Ryan's hand, not standard Tichu suits, but the three on the right wasn't quite standard and an odd symbol in a corner marked something different. It might have been Tichu.

Logan played a pair of tens and one of them slid across the table. Trevor slapped a hand down to catch it just before it went off the edge. The movement appeared practiced.

"I just wanted to play a game where no one complained about the cards being sticky or argued about which ones were stickier," Cameron said with a sigh. "The ones I ordered looked like normal Tichu cards, but this is what I got."

"Well, they're not sticky," Ryan said. He'd beaten the pair and was leading a straight. Though he set it down fanned out, the cards quickly slid on top of each other so that only the top one showed. He pushed them apart with his fingers. "It has eight cards."

"Sure it does," Logan said. He injected some sarcasm, but no one believed he doubted Ryan's word.

Trevor played a higher straight, after some of the cards fell out of his hand on the way to the table. He didn't say anything about that, though he looked as though he had a few things he wanted to say about it.

Logan was flipping through his cards to show the different faces to Audra. One of them fell into his lap, and he sighed as he retrieved it. The cards definitely did not have a stickiness problem. Violet wondered if the new problem was better. She found the guys' restraint regarding it amusing.

Cameron led a single, which Ryan caught before it escaped the table. He gently slid it back towards the center and Trevor still had to put a finger on it to keep it from going too far. A few other cards were played, carefully, before Logan played an ace. Ryan pulled out his odd card, and Violet saw a picture of a tiger on the front.

"What it that?" she asked.

He said, "The dragon."

"That's a tiger," Audra said.

"Pass," Trevor said. "It's also the dragon."

The other guys passed. Katie leaned forward to inspect the trick as Ryan collected it. "That's clearly a tiger," she said.

Ryan had played it like a dragon. He gave the cards to Logan, who repeatedly pushed at his stack of tricks that didn't want to stay stacked.

"We're pretending it's a dragon because it's the only dragon there is," Logan said.

"But it's a tiger," Audra said.

Katie picked up the box to examine it. "Does this version call it a tiger?"

"We don't know," Cameron told her. "The instructions are not in English."

She pulled out the paper curiously. Alison moved to look over her shoulder instead of Trevor's.

Trevor groaned slightly, with a gesture at Ryan and Violet behind him. "I hoped that with certain things settled, we could finally play a game without anyone being distracted. But now we have this tiger-shaped dragon stopping play."

"Oh, right." Ryan looked away from the foreign box and dropped his last cards on the table. The three kings split apart but stayed more or less in the center of the table.

Audra still looked puzzled. "Maybe you guys are playing the wrong game."

"Tichu is never the wrong game," Trevor said.

"And by the way, you're welcome," she added with a laugh.

Trevor squinted at her, then apparently decided not to ask what she meant.

Logan was more willing to humor her. "Why are we thanking you?"

"For getting *certain things* settled." She pointed at something in Logan's hand.

"Audra." Trevor's voice held the usual warning note about her giving things away.

"I'm just trying to get a better look at some of these weird cards," she said. "It doesn't have anything to do with the game. Exactly. But at least now Ryan is no longer allowed to give me a hard time about my poker face."

"You mean your lack of one?" Ryan asked.

She stared at him insolently. "That's right. All that time I was talking to you about Violet —"

"Pestering me, you mean."

"Every time I *talked* to you about Violet, I was thinking, 'Man, I hope he can't tell I know Violet is nuts about him.' And you couldn't tell."

"Hmm." The brief acknowledgment was the only response to Audra, but he glanced back at Violet for confirmation of the sentiment.

They shared a smile, having talked enough that it wasn't a surprise. Her eyes went to the others in the room and didn't see surprise anywhere. That didn't embarrass her anymore. She was in a room full of people who were all nuts about someone. It was wonderful to be included, wonderful to be surrounded by friendship while she found the best kind.

~~The End~~

Find out about upcoming books, read excerpts with notes from the author, watch various covers take shape, and much more at www.amandahammbooks.com.

www.ingramcontent.com/pod-product-compliance
Lightning Source LLC
Chambersburg PA
CBHW031345170626
46807CB00002B/829